GRANDPA'S MOUNTAIN

Other Avon Camelot Books by
Carolyn Reeder

SHADES OF GRAY

CAROLYN REEDER lives in a suburb of Washington, DC, only a few hours drive from the park described in this book. She has written one other book for young people, *Shades of Gray*.

Avon Books are available at special quantity discounts for bulk purchases for sales promotions, premiums, fund raising or educational use. Special books, or book excerpts, can also be created to fit specific needs.

For details write or telephone the office of the Director of Special Markets, Avon Books, Dept. FP, 1350 Avenue of the Americas, New York, NY 10019, 1-800-238-0658.

GRANDPA'S MOUNTAIN

CAROLYN REEDER

AN AVON CAMELOT BOOK

If you purchased this book without a cover, you should be aware that this book is stolen property. It was reported as "unsold and destroyed" to the publisher, and neither the author nor the publisher has received any payment for this "stripped book."

Grandpa's Mountain is fiction, and all its characters are fictitious. But much of the book is based on the true story of H.M. Cliser of Beahm, Virginia, who fought valiantly to save his home when land in the Blue Ridge Mountains was condemned to create Shenandoah National Park.

For my husband, Jack,
who introduced me to Shenandoah National Park
and who shares my love of its hiking trails,
its scenic beauty, and its fascinating history.

AVON BOOKS
A division of
The Hearst Corporation
1350 Avenue of the Americas
New York, New York 10019

Copyright © 1991 by Carolyn Reeder
Published by arrangement with Macmillan Publishing Company
Library of Congress Catalog Card Number: 90-27126
ISBN: 0-380-71914-2
RL: 5.0

All rights reserved, which includes the right to reproduce this book or portions thereof in any form whatsoever except as provided by the U.S. Copyright Law. For information address Macmillan Publishing Company, 833 Third Avenue, New York, New York 10022.

First Avon Camelot Printing: June 1993

CAMELOT TRADEMARK REG. U.S. PAT. OFF. AND IN OTHER COUNTRIES, MARCA REGISTRADA, HECHO EN U.S.A.

Printed in the U.S.A.

OPM 10 9 8 7 6 5 4 3

From the back seat of Grandpa's old Dodge, Carrie watched the green folds of the mountain ridges come closer and closer, until she was almost caught up in them. Pressing her face against the window, she watched eagerly for the summer's first glimpse of her grandparents' home. She held her breath as the car rounded the last hairpin curve and the white, two-story farmhouse came into sight.

It was just as she'd remembered it, with pots of red geraniums lining the wide front porch and hollyhocks blooming along the picket fence. And off to the right stood Grandpa's small general store with two gasoline pumps in front and Grandma's lunchroom beside it.

As soon as the car stopped, Carrie hurried to the yard, where Sport raced along the fence, wagging his long plume of a tail and barking frantically. Inside the gate she dropped to her knees and hugged the big black dog. "You didn't forget me, did you, boy?" she said, scratching his floppy ears while he tried to lick her face.

"I do believe that old dog's almost as glad to see you as we are!" Grandpa declared as he carried her suitcase to the house. Carrie's eyes followed his stocky figure, lingering on his thick shock of white hair.

Grandma paused to smile at Carrie on her way inside, and Carrie inhaled the faint lilac scent that always seemed to surround her grandmother's compact form. "We'll have an early supper," Grandma said, brushing back a strand of graying brown hair. "I know you're hungry after your train ride from the city."

Carrie gave Sport one last pat and got to her feet. "I'll help you," she said.

Grandma shook her head. "Go unpack and get yourself settled. You can help with the clearing up after supper."

Helping Grandma and Grandpa was one of the things Carrie liked best about summers in the mountains—it made her feel important and grown-up. When she tried to help at home, Mama always said, "Go on and play, Carrie. You'll have more than enough work in your lifetime." Her friends envied her because she didn't have chores to do, but Carrie felt useless and a little bit embarrassed.

Carrie followed Grandma inside. It was pleasantly cool; tall trees shaded the house, and a breeze stirred the white lace curtains. She climbed the stairs to her room and buried her face in the pink peonies on the bureau, breathing in their delicate fragrance. Glancing at her reflection as she turned away, Carrie hoped the summer sun would soon lighten her "dishwater blond" hair and give her pale skin a touch of color.

Quickly, she unpacked and took off her shoes. The wide boards of the floor were cool under her feet, their polished surface a contrast to the roughness of the rag rug. Pulling aside the curtain at the back window, she let her eyes rove from the weathered buildings behind the house to the garden with its neat green rows and then to the orchard beyond it. She couldn't see the pasture a neighbor rented from Grandpa, but she could hear the cattle lowing there.

It was just the way Carrie always thought of it when

she lost herself in summer memories to escape the topsy-turvy changes in her life at home. Nothing ever seemed to change here in Virginia's Blue Ridge Mountains. She loved the way summers with her grandparents were always the same—carefree days divided between helping Grandma and visiting with Kate and Luanne, her friends who lived up the road. And Sunday afternoons spent with her cousin Amanda. She could hardly wait to see Amanda again!

"I wish I could live here in the country all year," Carrie said, buttering one of Grandma's freshly baked biscuits.

"Oh, now, Carrie! Think how much you'd miss your Mama and Daddy!" Grandma said. Her gray eyes looked shocked.

But Grandpa agreed. "Right here on this mountain is the best possible place to live," he said emphatically. "I was born here and I intend to die here," he continued, accepting a second serving of fried chicken. "We work hard, and we don't owe anything. No matter what happens in this Depression, we'll be fine."

"Now, Claude, I'm sure Carrie doesn't want to talk about the Depression," Grandma said.

Carrie stared down at her plate. She didn't even want to *think* about it. She wanted to forget the months and months her father had been out of work, and how quickly the hopeful look left Mama's face each evening when he came home and sank listlessly into his chair, mumbling, "Nothing today, either." She wanted to forget how they'd had to move to an even smaller apartment, and how hard it had been to change schools in the middle of the year and to make friends in the new neighborhood. She even wanted to forget what life at home was like now that Daddy finally had found a job. He worked at night and needed to sleep during the day, so she had to remember to tiptoe and whisper, and her friends couldn't visit anymore. Worst of all, she saw Daddy only at suppertime, and the evenings alone with Mama seemed so long and dreary. . . .

Grandpa's voice brought her back to the present. "No, Sarah, I think it's important for Carrie to know that we're safe from the Depression here. We can't lose our house or the store, because there's no mortgage on either one of them. And we'll always have plenty to eat because of the garden and your flock of chickens. The future looks pretty good to me."

"To me, too," Carrie said, thinking of the long, peaceful summer stretching before her.

The next morning Carrie woke to the sound of Grandma's roosters crowing and the smell of bacon frying. She rolled out of bed, slipped into her clothes, and ran a comb through her short curls before hurrying down to the kitchen.

"Good morning, Sunshine!" Grandma said, flipping a pancake. "And what are you going to do today?"

"Everything!" Carrie said, beaming with pleasure at the sound of the pet name her grandparents had given her years before. "I'm going to do everything I always do here. First, I'll help you bake pies for the lunchroom, and then

I'll walk up the road and see Kate and Luanne. This afternoon, I'll go down and see Annie Burns—"

"That's Mrs. Burns, Carrie," Grandma said sternly.

"Mrs. Burns," Carrie said quickly, though she always thought of her grandparents' elderly neighbors as Sam and Annie. "And this evening I'll help Grandpa close up the store," she went on, thinking of the jars of penny candies lining the counter.

"You can go on down to the post office for me after you leave the Burns place," Grandma said, handing Carrie a platter of pancakes. "Old Mrs. Sly doesn't have that dog anymore."

Carrie didn't know what to say. Ever since she could remember, she'd begged not to be sent to the post office because Mrs. Sly's dog barked and snarled at her when she went past. But it wasn't really the dog she feared—it was Frank Benton, the postmistress's older son. Frank always found something to taunt Carrie about, and she hated the tongue-tied, helpless way he made her feel.

"Nobody was sorry when that old dog disappeared," Grandma went on. "And nobody's sorry that Frank's gone, either."

"Frank's gone?" Carrie's heart leaped.

Grandma nodded. "Mr. Benton caught him throwing rocks at cars and decided he needed something to keep him out of trouble. So he packed him off to work on his uncle's farm in the valley till school starts."

Carrie drew a deep breath. With Frank Benton gone, this should be a perfect summer!

* * *

By the end of the day, Carrie had done everything she'd planned, and more. Swaying gently on the porch swing beside Grandma as the twilight deepened, the last line of Mama's favorite poem popped into Carrie's head.

"All's right with the world," she said, not caring at all that the poem was about morning, or that very little was right with the world she knew in Washington, D.C. Her summers in the mountains were a perfect world of their own.

"All's right with *our* world, anyway," Grandma said, smiling.

2

Carrie knelt in front of the dining room window and rested her folded arms on the sill, watching for her aunt's family to arrive for Sunday dinner. Grandma had banished her from the kitchen, saying, "They'll be here when they get here, child. Now, shoo!"

At last a farm truck turned off the road and came to a stop by the fence. Before Aunt Rose and Uncle George were out of the cab, Amanda, Clarence, and Benjamin had climbed over the wooden sides of the truck bed and jumped to the ground. Amanda was still wearing her chestnut-colored hair in braids, Carrie noticed as she ran toward the gate.

"How's my favorite niece?" Aunt Rose asked, hugging her.

"Fine," Carrie replied, smiling shyly. Aunt Rose sounded so much like Mama that Carrie felt a pang of homesickness, but she shook it off and headed for the front porch with Amanda. Carrie saw that they were still almost exactly the same height, even though she was eleven and her cousin had just turned ten. She straightened her shoulders and held her head high, hoping she'd look taller.

The porch swing was Carrie and Amanda's favorite spot. But no sooner had they settled down to talk than Clarence wedged himself between them and little Benjamin climbed onto Carrie's lap.

"Why don't you two go play with Sport?" suggested Amanda.

Both boys shook their heads.

"But Carrie and I want to talk!"

"Go ahead and talk, then," said Clarence.

And Benjamin snuggled into a more comfortable position, echoing happily, "Go ahead and talk."

"How can we talk with you here?" Amanda asked, her voice rising.

"Carrie doesn't want us to leave, do you, Carrie?" asked Clarence.

His wide brown eyes looked innocent, but Carrie knew how much he enjoyed tormenting his older sister. "Of course I don't want you to leave, Clarence," she said. "You and Benjamin can sit here as long as you like." And then she turned to Amanda and said, "*Eeway ancay alktay ithway emthay erehay.*"

Amanda's face lit up. "I *orgotfay!*" she said. "*Eeway—*"

But before she could go on, Clarence stood up and said

with disgust, "Come on, Benjamin. Let's go find Sport."

"You're so clever, Carrie!" said Amanda. "Why didn't I think of that? But we'd better whisper, because if I know Clarence, he'll be sneaking around to spy on us."

It wasn't long before Grandma called them to dinner. Carrie looked around the table with satisfaction. She always enjoyed the leisurely Sunday meal with everyone catching up on the latest news.

After the platters of ham and fried chicken and the bowls of vegetables had been passed around the table, Aunt Rose turned to Grandpa. "Dad, did George tell you what he heard in town yesterday?" she asked.

"Can't say that he did," Grandpa said, looking inquiringly at his son-in-law. "What's the latest news in Luray, George?"

Uncle George looked uncomfortable. "Well, it's more of a rumor," he said. "I—I'd rather not be spreading it."

Aunt Rose started to say something, but Grandma gave her a warning look. "George is right," she said. "We shouldn't borrow trouble. If it's true, we'll read about it in the county paper soon enough."

"Forewarned is forearmed, I always say," Aunt Rose answered. Then she turned to Grandpa. "Dad, there's talk about a plan to have a national park along the Blue Ridge all the way from Front Royal almost to Waynesboro. If it works out, you could lose this place."

Lose this place? Shocked, Carrie looked from Aunt Rose to Grandpa.

"There's been talk like that off and on for years, Rose, but it's nothing to worry about," Grandpa said reassuringly.

"Hundreds of families live in these mountains, don't forget, and national parks are wild, natural places. Places with spectacular scenery, like Yellowstone and the Grand Canyon."

Places in the West, Carrie thought, feeling as though a heavy weight had been lifted off her chest. She'd seen pictures of Old Faithful and a view of the Grand Canyon in her geography book. There certainly wasn't anything like that here in the Virginia mountains!

Aunt Rose leaned forward. "But Dad, a story like this doesn't just spring up from nowhere! There's bound to be some truth in it, especially if it's been around for a while."

Carrie felt a stab of fear. What if Aunt Rose was right?

"Probably that Skyland resort up there's going to be expanded and somebody misunderstood and blew things all out of proportion. You know how people are, Rose. Now, would somebody please pass me that ham?"

Aunt Rose pressed her lips together in a thin line, the same way Mama did when she disapproved of something. For a moment, Carrie felt a little sorry for her aunt. She knew how it felt to be brushed off when you had something important to say. But she was glad Aunt Rose had told Grandpa the rumor. It was terrible not to know what was going on—Grandpa would probably hate that just as much as she did.

Soon everyone was talking and laughing again, and Carrie was relieved that the Sunday visit hadn't been spoiled. When dinner was over, the girls helped clear the table and then went upstairs. They sprawled across Carrie's bed, whispering and giggling until Aunt Rose called that it

RARY

was time to leave. Then they stood in front of the calendar that hung on Carrie's wall and counted the number of visits they would have that summer.

"I wish you could come every Sunday instead of just every other week," Carrie said.

"So do I, but we have to visit our other grandparents, too," Amanda reminded her.

"I know, but I still don't think it's fair that your cousins in Harrisonburg get to see you all year 'round but I'll only see you five more times this summer."

"We'll have a whole week together when you come to the farm at the end of August. And it'll be six more times before that, Carrie—don't forget about the Fourth of July. Ooh, I can hardly wait! Don't you wish it was tomorrow?"

Carrie loved the Fourth of July celebration in town, but she could wait. She wasn't about to wish away more than two weeks of her summer in the mountains.

3

From the kitchen window, Carrie saw Mr. Albert's delivery truck jerk to a stop outside the store. She watched him jump out and take the steps two at a time. He hurried inside without even speaking to the two old men who were sitting on the porch, talking.

Carrie frowned. Mr. Albert wasn't due until the next day. Besides, he obviously hadn't come to bring Grandpa sacks of chicken feed. Why had he come? And why was he in such a hurry? Carrie was proud that Grandma had left her to start the baking by herself when some travelers stopped at the lunchroom, but she really wanted to know what was happening at the store. Wiping the flour from her hands, she took off her apron and slipped out the door. The pies would have to wait.

She ran over to the store, slowing when she reached the steps, and heard her grandfather shouting inside. The old men on the porch had stopped their own conversation to listen.

"I don't believe a word of it! Why, it's against the Constitution, that's what it is!"

And then she heard Mr. Albert say, "It's true, Claude. Go see for yourself. The newspaper office has a copy of the map."

Carrie flattened herself against the front of the store as Grandpa burst out the door and hurried down the steps and around the house toward the car shed. Grandma came out of the lunchroom to see what was happening. Carrie joined her, and they watched Grandpa drive around the house, pull out onto the road, and head toward town. Mr. Albert stood in front of the store and watched, too, shaking his head. Then, mumbling something about being behind schedule, he climbed into his truck and drove away.

Carrie looked up at her grandmother. "Grandma, what—"

"Go back and finish the pies, Carrie," Grandma said in a firm voice. "I'm down to my last two slices."

Carrie cut the lard into the flour and rolled the dough for the pie crusts, but her mind wasn't on her work. What had Mr. Albert told Grandpa that made him drive off toward town to see a map? And why didn't Grandma want to talk about it?

The pies were out of the oven and Carrie was shelling peas for dinner when she saw Grandma coming toward the house. Carrie went out to meet her. Now maybe she'd find out what was going on.

"When those pies are cool, take them on over to the lunchroom. And keep an eye out for customers—you'll have to wait on anybody who comes while I'm minding the store for your Grandpa."

"What do you think is wrong?" Carrie asked. When Grandma pressed her lips together and didn't answer, Carrie suddenly felt cold all over. "Grandma, do you suppose—"

"I don't suppose anything, Carrie," Grandma said, turning away. "We'll know for sure soon enough."

After she took the pies over, Carrie stayed at the lunchroom, and in the long stretches of time between customers, she stood at the screen door and watched for Grandpa's car. Where could he have gone? The sound of laughter made her glance toward the store. The group of farmers who congregated to exchange local news and talk about the weather was larger than usual, she noticed.

It was mid-afternoon before the old Dodge turned off the road and disappeared around the side of the house. And it was several minutes more before Grandpa appeared. Carrie slipped out of the lunchroom and ran over to the store to join her grandmother. Together, they stood just inside the screen door, waiting to see what would happen.

The men on the porch grew silent when they saw

Grandpa striding toward them. At the foot of the steps, he stopped and surveyed them grimly. "Nero fiddled while Rome burned," he said, "and we've been talking and joking while plans were being made to take our homes."

Carrie gasped, thinking back to Sunday dinner.

There was a murmur of voices, and an old man asked, "What are you sayin', Claude? Who's gonna take our homes?"

"You needn't worry, Clem," drawled a younger man. "Nobody'd want your place."

The burst of laughter died down when Grandpa said, "You won't think it's so funny when the government makes you leave your farms!"

"You'd better start at the beginning, Claude," said a tall, thin man who was sitting on a wooden box, whittling.

Grandpa looked from man to man. When he was sure he had everyone's attention, he began. "The government in Washington wants to have a new national park—and they're going to put it right along these mountains. Right along the Blue Ridge. They want it to be a place where city people from all over the East can come and enjoy nature. Where they can see trees and wild animals." He spit on the ground.

A voice broke the stunned silence. "I remember hearing some talk about a park a while back, but they was going to put it up at that Skyland place, where that feller has the summer resort."

"It'll be at Skyland, all right," Grandpa told him. "And it'll be at Kemp Hollow and Jewell Hollow—yes, Jim, it'll be at Jewell Hollow. It'll be at Beahms Gap, too. And along the Buracker Road," he said, his eyes falling on one man and then another. "And the Price Lands. You're a tenant on the Price Lands, aren't you, Tom?" he asked another man.

The man nodded slowly.

"They want to take the farm of every man here, and they want to take this place, too!" His voice shook with anger.

Grandma's hand closed on Carrie's arm. "Then what George heard wasn't a rumor! Rose was right—we really are in danger of losing our home!"

Carrie's mouth was so dry she couldn't answer. No wonder Uncle George hadn't wanted to tell Grandpa about this on Sunday!

"But your place is right on the road, Claude," protested a bearded man. "Wouldn't make no sense to have a park on a paved road like this one."

"When I was in town just now I saw the map," Grandpa said. "All the houses from the old road to the mill on across the mountains are on land they want to take for the new park. For Shenandoah National Park." His voice was scornful.

The men on the porch stirred uneasily, and Grandma slipped a comforting arm around Carrie's waist.

"You can sit here and take this if you want to," Grandpa said, "but I'm going to fight it. I'm a Virginian and an American, and I've got the Declaration of Independence and the U.S. Constitution behind me." He glared at the silent men for a moment before he turned and headed toward the house.

One by one, the men left the store porch. A few

lingered near the gas pumps, talking, and the rest started soberly for home.

"Let's go back to the house," said Grandma. She pulled the heavy wooden door shut and locked it, and Carrie hung the CLOSED sign from a nail on the screen. She couldn't remember ever closing the store in the middle of the afternoon before.

Grandpa looked up when they came into the kitchen. "This is the only home I've ever known, and I don't aim to give it up!" he declared, banging his fist on the table.

"But what are you going to do, Grandpa?" asked Carrie.

His blue eyes blazed under his bushy white eyebrows. "I'm going to write a letter to the editor calling for all the landowners to join together and fight to save our homes."

"We'll have an early supper," Grandma said, getting up, "and then you can work on it. Carrie, go out to the garden and pick me some lettuce while I start cooking those peas you shelled this morning."

As Carrie pinched off the largest leaves from the lettuce plants, her head was whirling. This was Grandpa's land—Griffins had lived here for more than a hundred years. How could the government suddenly decide to take it away from them? She took a deep breath and said aloud, "Grandpa won't let them do it." Her fear and confusion gave way to a calm feeling of confidence, and she started back to the house.

Later that evening Grandpa announced, "I'm going down to talk to Sam Burns now that I've finished my letter."

"Can I come, too?" asked Carrie. She wanted to hear what Grandpa and Sam would say about the new park.

"Sure," he said. "Come on."

They walked along the edge of the road until they came to the Burns place. Sam and Annie were sitting on the porch.

"Hey, Claude," called Sam. "Glad you stopped by!"

Annie Burns smiled at Carrie. "Come help me fix some lemonade and cake, dear," she said.

When they returned with the refreshments, the men were deep in talk. "I don't like the idea of Washington using my tax money to buy up my neighbors' land for a park for city slickers," Sam was saying.

Grandpa reached for a glass on Carrie's tray. "I learned in town today that it's Virginia, not the United States government, that's actually buying the land. The legislature's passed a law to let the state condemn thousands and thousands of acres in one fell swoop. Our representative is going to have to answer for this!"

"But if it's going to be a *national* park—" began Sam.

"Once it's bought up all the land, Virginia's going to donate it to the U. S. government," Grandpa explained.

"Where will Virginia get the money?" Carrie asked.

"The legislature's voted a million dollars toward buying the land, and some of the city folks have been making contributions, too," Grandpa said, turning toward her. "People in Richmond and Charlottesville—even people in Washington, D.C.—have given money for the park. Why, a man in town told me that anybody who'd give six dollars got a certificate saying they'd bought an acre of Shenandoah National Park."

"Six dollars an acre!" Sam snorted. "Maybe for some rocky mountaintop, but not for cultivated land along a paved road!"

"At that rate, my forty-five acres would bring two hundred seventy dollars. And I've got—well, you know what I've got," Grandpa said.

"You'll get twenty or thirty times that," Sam said. "The government will have to pay you what it's worth."

"The government couldn't afford to pay what that place is worth to me," Grandpa said quietly.

Carrie stirred uneasily. She liked it better when Grandpa was angry, when he banged his fist on the table.

They all sat silently for a while, watching the fireflies blink in the growing darkness. Wistfully, Carrie thought of how she used to run after them and remembered the way the cool, greenish light glowed between her clasped fingers when she caught one.

Finally Grandpa stood up. "We'd best be getting home," he said. "Much obliged for the cake and lemonade, Annie."

That night Carrie lay awake for a long time. She could hear the flutter of insect wings against her window screens and the whippoorwill's repetitive call from the orchard. She put the feather pillow over her ears to block out the sounds so she could think.

What if Grandpa couldn't save this place? she wondered. What would happen to him and Grandma? And what about her own Blue Ridge Mountain summers?

Suddenly Carrie sat up in bed. What was the matter with her, anyway? How could she have forgotten what Grandpa said at suppertime? This had always been his home, and he would never give it up. Reassured, she lay back and closed her eyes.

4

After dinner on Sunday, Grandpa said, "Sarah, I'm going up on the ridge to talk with Clive Hopkins and another farmer I know. Why don't you and Carrie ride along with me?"

Driving up the mountain, they passed the Wards' large house with its four brick chimneys and then the one-room schoolhouse with its blank, staring windows and the words MOUNTAIN VIEW SCHOOL painted over the door. Kate and Luanne's house, a row of rocking chairs lining the porch, was next. Carrie wished she could spend the afternoon with her girlfriends instead of visiting people she didn't know.

Just before they reached the crest of the mountain, Grandpa turned onto a narrow dirt road. As they drove past the small farms on either side, he shook his head and said, "You tell me what will become of these people if they're run off their land."

Finally he pulled off the road and parked by a barn. Clive Hopkins came to meet them, and his wife, Betty, called for Grandma and Carrie to join her on the porch. Three small boys, fingers in their mouths, stood beside their mother and stared at the visitors. But Clara, a thin, dark-haired girl who looked about Carrie's age, smiled shyly. Carrie smiled back, wishing she could think of something to say.

"Well, Sarah," said Mrs. Hopkins, lifting the smallest child onto her lap, "what do you think about this park business?"

Grandma's eyes narrowed. "I don't want to give up my home to make a play place for city folk."

Mrs. Hopkins nodded sympathetically. "I can understand how you'd feel that way," she said. "You've got such a nice home. A shingled house, and running water, and the electric." She sighed. "I've always been a great admirer of the electric."

Grandma leaned forward, her gray eyes earnest. "Are you saying you'd be willing to give up this place? The place Clive brought you to as a bride and where all your children were born?" When Mrs. Hopkins didn't answer, Grandma went on. "And what about the two little ones buried not a stone's throw from where we're sitting? If you leave here, those graves will be grown over with brambles in no time at all!"

Mrs. Hopkins turned to Clara. "Why don't you take Carrie out to the barn and show her the kittens," she suggested. "You'd like that, wouldn't you, Carrie?"

"Yes, ma'am," Carrie answered politely, although she wished she could stay on the porch and listen to the women talk. She hadn't realized that the homes farther up the mountain didn't have running water or electricity. She'd never thought about babies dying, either.

The younger children dashed for the barn, and Clara and Carrie followed. "The kittens just got their eyes open yesterday," Clara said.

"How many are there?" Carrie asked, glad for something to talk about.

"Six. You can hold one."

Inside the barn, Clara shooed her brothers away from the mother cat and her litter. "You all go over there," she said, pointing to the opposite corner. "Me and Carrie are going to play with the kittens by ourselves."

Carrie picked up a tiny gray kitten and stroked its soft fur.

The men's voices drifted in. "I'd like to stay put," Clive was saying. "This place has been in my family four generations. But Betty, she wants to go."

"You going to let her decide that?" Grandpa sounded so skeptical that Carrie had to smile.

"Always before, when she'd talk about leaving, I'd tell her we'd go if we could find a buyer. I knew nobody'd come asking to buy this place." Clive paused. "But now I've got a buyer—and I can't go back on my word, Claude. Besides, with the money we get from the state, I figure we can buy us a place in the valley."

"I just can't see you as a flatlander, Clive."

Carrie could picture Grandpa shaking his head in disbelief.

"Won't be all bad, you know," Clive went on. "The young'ns will have better schooling, and we'll be able to get a doctor when we need one. It was right hard on Betty, losing the baby and little Rachel to diphtheria 'cause we couldn't get word to Doc Rich in time. You know, Claude, living there right on the paved road, you don't know what we're up against back here."

"The road in didn't seem all that bad to me."

"It probably don't seem nearly as far when you drive in as when you have to walk it, either. Now come on out to the field," he said, changing the subject, "and take a look at my buckwheat crop."

The men's voices faded away and Carrie asked, "Do you want to leave the mountains, Clara?"

Clara nodded. "Mama says life's a lot easier in the valley. And I'll be able to go to school the whole term. When it's rainy or real cold, Mama don't let me walk out to the paved road."

"You mean you have to walk all the way to the Mountain View School?" Carrie asked in surprise.

Clara nodded again. Then she whispered, "Do you suppose those valley kids will laugh at me 'cause I don't read so good?"

"I—I don't know," Carrie said, adding quickly, "but you'll probably catch on fast once you're going to school every day."

The little boys, who had slipped out of the barn while the girls were talking, came running in. "Her grandma says she should come on now," one of them shouted, and then they turned and ran out again.

Clara and Carrie gently put the kittens back on the straw and watched them snuggle up beside their mother.

•   •   •

In the car again, Grandma said, "Betty Hopkins wants Clive to sell to the state and buy a place in the valley. She said two families she knows have already sold and plan to move away next week."

"They're some of the lucky ones that own their farms," Grandpa said. "But Clive told me over half the people in these mountains don't own the land they live on. I'm hoping Gus Smith can give me some more information."

The road was narrower now, scarcely more than a wagon track, and Grandpa had to drive slowly because of all the rocks. Carrie was glad when he finally stopped the car by a split-rail fence at the edge of a clearing and said, "We have to walk from here." She climbed out of the car and took deep breaths of the honeysuckle-scented air. Then she followed her grandparents into a pasture where cattle raised their heads and stared at them as they walked by.

They headed across the pasture toward a small house with a tin roof that glinted in the afternoon sun. "Gus Smith is a tenant farmer for the valley man who owns this grazing land and all these cows," he told Carrie. "He keeps the fences repaired and sees that the cows have the salt they need, and for his pay, he and his wife get to use the house and land."

Carrie nodded. She already knew what tenant farmers were, but she liked the way Grandpa always made sure she didn't feel left out of the conversation.

"But, Claude," Grandma said, "Since Gus is a tenant, that means the landowner in the valley will get the money if the state takes this land! What will become of Gus and his wife?"

Before Grandpa could answer, a stooped little man came to meet them. "Howdy, Gus," Grandpa said, introducing Carrie.

Gus nodded politely to her and Grandma. "Come on up to the house and set with Minnie," he said.

"I'm right glad you stopped by," Mrs. Smith said as Carrie and Grandma climbed the steps to the porch. "We don't get many visitors way back here. Since all my girls married, I've been right lonesome."

"You should ride along with Gus when he comes to the store," Grandma said, seating herself in a rocking chair. "You could keep me company in the lunchroom."

Mrs. Smith shook her head sadly. "We don't have no wagon any more, and there's just one horse," she said, gesturing toward an old roan mare leaning over the fence, trying to reach the tall grass on the other side.

Carrie hoped the women would talk about the new park, but instead Mrs. Smith began to complain about her rheumatism. After a few minutes, Carrie slipped away from the porch and walked toward the fence. The mare lifted her head and Carrie whispered, "Hello, pretty lady." Tentatively, she patted the horse's nose. Then she stroked her neck and fed her bunches of grass and clover. The feel of the delicate lips on her palm made her shiver with delight.

All too soon, Mrs. Smith called from the porch. "Tell ol' Nelly good-bye and come on up, Carrie. I'm going to fix us a dish of peach cobbler."

"Be sure you fix some for us, too," Gus Smith said as he and Grandpa came around the corner of the house. "Yessir," he said, turning back to Grandpa, "if this park plan goes through, I'll be mighty pleased. It'll give me a chance to have my own land instead of just workin' on somebody else's."

"And there'll be neighbors," added his wife, coming out with the dishes of cobbler.

Carrie frowned. Were Grandma and Grandpa the only ones who didn't want to leave the mountains?

"Most of the homesteads will be only fifteen acres, so the houses can't be too far apart," Gus agreed.

Homesteads? What was he talking about? Carrie wondered.

"I just hope there's decent roads so I can get to church on preachin' Sunday and to the store once in a while," said Mrs. Smith. "Do you know, Sarah, I can't even remember the last time I picked out my own dress material. I guess I'm lucky Gus has such fine taste, ain't I?"

They all laughed, but Carrie knew that Grandma always went over to the store to help when a mountain man wanted dress goods for his wife.

On the way back to the car, Grandpa told them what he'd learned from Gus. "Seems like the government in Washington won't accept the land from Virginia till plans are made to provide for the families that have to leave."

Grandma frowned. "But who's going to provide for all those people?"

"Gus says the government's organized a program to

relocate them. Some officials have bought big tracts of land and divided them into small farms—homesteads, they're calling them—for people who can't afford to buy a new place."

Carrie interrupted him. "But how will they afford to build a house, even if the land is free?" she asked.

"That's the amazing thing," Grandpa answered. "Each family will have a house built for them, and a barn, too. And everything else they'll need to start farming."

"Won't that be wonderful for Gus and Minnie!" exclaimed Grandma. Then she said, "You know, Claude, it looks to me like a lot of people don't feel the way we do about having their places bought up for this park."

"Not the folks we've seen today, anyhow," Grandpa agreed reluctantly. "They seem to be glad to leave."

Carrie didn't blame them. She certainly wouldn't want to live way back here with only cattle for company. Not even if she had a horse like Nelly. She followed her grandparents back across the pasture and climbed into the car for the slow, jolting trip on the old wagon track.

Carrie rolled down the dusty window. Now she could see the summer wildflowers along the faint roadway and the tall oaks and maples on either side. Even the gray skeletons of the blight-killed chestnut trees had a kind of somber beauty.

"I can imagine this being a park," she said suddenly as they came into another clearing and she saw the mountain peaks silhouetted against the rosy evening sky. "But how can anybody imagine *our* place being a park?"

5

Carrie had just come back from visiting Kate and Luanne when a large brown truck stopped at the gas pumps and men dressed in blue denim uniforms climbed out of the back. A few went up the steps to the store, but most of them headed for the lunchroom. Carrie hurried over to help Grandma, and by the time she got there the counter and all three tables were full.

"Quick, start cutting those pies," Grandma said when Carrie slipped behind the counter and reached for her apron. "We'll have to bake again this afternoon—these CCC boys are going to clean us out."

"You mean this little girl helped bake all them cherry pies?" asked one of the men. "Why, I just might have to marry her!"

Carrie's face reddened, but she didn't look up.

"Aw, you're too old for her, Paul. She'd be a lot better off marryin' me," teased his friend.

"Can she bake a cherry pie, Billy Boy, Billy Boy?" sang one of the men, and another held his plate high and sang back in a sweet, tenor voice, "She can bake a cherry pie quick as a cat can wink its eye! But she's a young thing, and cannot leave her mother!"

Carrie's hand shook as she lifted a piece of pie onto a plate, and she felt hot with embarrassment. She was grateful when Grandma came to her rescue.

"If you boys want pie," she said sternly, sweeping her

eyes along the row of young men seated at the counter, "there'll be no more talk of marrying my assistant baker."

There were murmurs of "Yes, ma'am" and "No offense meant," and then the men began to talk among themselves as they ate. Soon they—and all the pies—were gone.

As Grandma and Carrie collected the dirty dishes and cutlery, Carrie asked, "Who are those CCC boys, anyway?"

"They're part of the Civilian Conservation Corps," Grandma replied. "It's run like the army, but instead of fighting, the men work to protect our natural resources."

"I thought natural resources were coal, and oil, and things like that," Carrie said, puzzled.

"Forests are natural resources, too. I think this group's been brought in to help develop that new national park."

Carrie didn't want to think about the national park. "I never heard of the CCC before," she said.

"It's new," Grandma explained. "It's one of President Roosevelt's ideas to help young men who can't get jobs because of the Depression and to help the country at the same time. I read about it in the paper. Now let's take care of these dishes so we can start another batch of pies."

That evening at supper, Grandma said, "With the CCC stopping by, I made more money in the lunchroom today than I usually make in a week."

Grandpa scowled. "We got along fine without their business," he said. "And the city slickers got along fine without the trails and picnic grounds those fellows are so proud of building up there on the ridge. I've got a mind to put a sign that says, CCC Not Welcome Here."

"They're just doing their job, Claude," Grandma said mildly. "They're young men away from home for the first time, most of them. It won't hurt us any to let them buy a little candy and tobacco, or a cup of coffee and a piece of homemade pie."

Grandpa leaned forward. "You know what part of their job is, Sarah? When a family up on the mountain sells their land for the park, the CCC moves all their stuff to their new place for them."

"That's right accommodating," Grandma said.

"After you hear what one of those boys told me, you might not think they're quite so 'accommodating.' Soon as the people leave, they destroy everything. They set fire to the house and barn and all the other buildings and burn 'em to the ground!"

"Why do they do that?" Carrie cried.

Grandpa's blue eyes blazed. "So they can't change their minds and move back, I guess. Besides, it wouldn't do to have the tourists know that somebody used to live there when they come to spend their vacation in the national park, would it?" He threw down his napkin and left the table.

Carrie stared down at her plate. She didn't feel like eating any more, either.

Grandma sighed. "Poor man can't think of anything but this park business. I've never seen him so worried."

"Don't you worry, too?" Carrie asked, looking up.

Grandma sighed again. Her forehead was creased with

lines Carrie had never noticed before. "What will be will be," she said, "and worrying isn't going to make a bit of difference."

"Grandpa thinks he'll be able to change things. Don't you think he can?"

"I don't know, Carrie. I really don't. But I certainly hope so."

"Well, I'm sure Grandpa will find a way for us to stay here," Carrie said firmly.

A few minutes later Grandpa called from the front porch. "Sarah, Carrie, we've got company!"

Carrie and Grandma hurried to the door in time to see Sam and Annie Burns coming in the gate.

"Have you seen this yet?" called Sam, waving a copy of the weekly county newspaper.

Grandpa shook his head. "Plan to get mine tomorrow morning when I go in to the bank."

Sam tossed him the paper, and he and Annie seated themselves on the porch swing. "They printed your letter to the editor."

Carrie hung over Grandpa's and Grandma's shoulders to read it.

To the Editor:

A man's home is his castle, and he has every right to feel secure in it. Now that the homes of hundreds of us freedom-loving Virginians are threatened with condemnation for this Shenandoah National Park, we must band together to oppose the unconstitutional seizure of our property. First, we must . . .

When they'd finished reading, Grandpa refolded the paper neatly and handed it back to Sam. "I wrote that last week, when I first heard about this park business. Things seem a little different now," he said gruffly.

"I thought what you said about everyone joining together to hire a lawyer was the best part," Carrie said enthusiastically.

"So did I," Annie Burns agreed, smiling at her.

Grandpa leaned toward Sam. "When I wrote that," he said earnestly, "I thought everyone felt like I do. I thought everyone would object to being forced to leave these mountains." He sighed and leaned back. "Well, now I've found out that some of the folks up on the ridge are glad for a chance to move away."

"Is that so?" asked Sam.

Grandpa nodded. "They have dreams of running water and electricity and better schools for their youngsters."

"Well, those things never hurt us," Sam said.

Carrie suppressed a giggle, but Grandpa went on as if he hadn't heard Sam's comment.

"So I guess the thing to do now is organize the people who live along the road here."

"What exactly do you have in mind, Claude?" asked Sam.

Grandpa leaned forward again. "If all of us work together, we ought to be able to get the park boundary moved far enough back from the road that we can keep our land. What do you think, Sam?"

The rhythmic squeaking of the porch swing filled the silence until Sam finally said, "I think you'd better find out how people 'round here feel before you write any more letters."

Sam didn't think it would work, Carrie realized with a jolt. But Grandpa could do it, no matter what Sam, or anybody else, thought.

Grandma stood up. "Carrie and I baked this afternoon. Come on in and we'll all have some cherry pie."

"Don't mind if I do," Sam said, winking at Carrie. "Don't mind if I do."

6

"What exactly is 'politicking,' Grandpa?" Carrie asked as they walked up the road the next evening.

"Why, it's influencing people to feel the same way you do, Sunshine."

Carrie frowned. Last night Sam Burns had told Grandpa he ought to find out how the other people along the road felt about the park business, but "going politicking" didn't sound like quite the same thing.

"Aren't you going to talk to the Wards?" Carrie asked when Grandpa walked right past their front gate.

"The Wards have choir practice Thursday evenings. We'll start with Hugh Edwards and go on from there."

That suited Carrie just fine—she'd have longer to visit with Kate and Luanne. When they drew near the Edwards place, Carrie saw her friends and their older brother, Moses, in the yard. Tommy, the youngest of the family, was sitting on the porch playing near his parents. The girls waved and called to Carrie, and Moses looked up and grinned. He was turning the crank of the ice-cream freezer, and Carrie found herself watching his muscles flex as he worked.

"C'mon, Carrie, let's jump Double Dutch till the ice cream's ready," Kate called. "You can be first." The sisters took their places along the narrow sidewalk that led from the gate to the porch steps, one end of a rope in each hand. As though at some unseen signal, they began to turn the ropes in opposite directions. The gentle slope of the sidewalk made the girls seem the same height, and with their blue eyes and long flaxen braids they looked almost like twins.

Carrie stood poised on the grass, sensing the rhythm of the two ropes and waiting for the right moment to jump in. It didn't bother her a bit that Moses was watching. Double Dutch was something she was good at.

Lightly, she ran onto the sidewalk and began to jump. She loved the *slap, slap, slap* of the ropes on the concrete and the symmetrical arcs that rose and fell around her. And she loved the way her hair bounced. She could almost feel the curls tightening up, as tiny beads of perspiration gathered along her forehead.

"Engine, engine, number nine, running on Chicago line," chanted Kate and Luanne. "If the train should jump the track, do you want your money—"

But suddenly Carrie heard Grandpa's voice above the chanting, and her feet faltered and became tangled in the rope.

"What kind of man are you, Edwards, to take this lying down?"

Mr. Edwards' voice was angry. "It's all very well for you to talk! You've nothing to lose and everything to gain."

"What have you got to lose by signing?" Grandpa asked.

"My job! I don't want to leave here any more than you do, but I'd rather move than lose my job. I've signed on to help build that road through the park, so the state's paying my salary!"

"That's no reason to lie down and roll over and let the government take your home away from you," Grandpa argued.

Carrie gasped as Mr. Edwards crumpled the petition in his huge hand and stood up, towering over Grandpa. "Get out of here, Griffin. Just get out!" he shouted, shaking his fist.

With great dignity, Grandpa stood up, too. He nodded toward Mrs. Edwards and started down the porch steps. The three girls, who had been watching, openmouthed, moved off the sidewalk and he walked past them without speaking. Carrie saw that his jaw was set with anger.

"I—I'd better go," she said, embarrassed. The girls nodded, looking fearfully toward the porch where Mr. Edwards stood with his fists clenched, his feet firmly planted, and his huge belly hanging over his belt. No wonder Kate and Luanne were afraid of him, Carrie thought. Before she turned toward the gate, she noticed Tommy standing beside his father, glaring after Grandpa.

As she left, Carrie glanced over at Moses. He looked troubled, but he managed a wry smile and a shrug. The ice cream must be almost ready now, she realized, noticing how slowly Moses was cranking.

The gate swung shut behind her, and Carrie hurried to catch up with Grandpa. When she fell into step beside him he muttered, "I was sure Hugh Edwards would sign." He didn't seem to expect an answer, so Carrie walked along silently, nursing her feelings of embarrassment and disappointment. She gave a start when Grandpa said, "I'd have saved the draft of that petition if I'd thought anybody'd react like Edwards did. It's going to take me till bedtime to write it over again."

"You're still going to try to get people to sign it?" Carrie asked in surprise.

"Of course! You can't let a little setback discourage you."

A little setback! "But Mr. Edwards was almost violent! What if—"

Grandpa rested his hand on Carrie's shoulder. "The United States Constitution guarantees my right to petition, and there isn't anybody on this mountain—or anywhere else—that's going to keep me from exercising that right. We'll go to the Wards' house after supper tomorrow."

"I think I'll stay home tomorrow night, Grandpa. I don't really like politicking."

*   *   *

It was after dark the next night when Grandpa came back home. Carrie could tell from the way he walked that things hadn't gone well, and she wondered if the other neighbors were angry at him now, too.

"Did you have better luck this evening, Claude?" Grandma asked.

"I got a couple of signatures," he said, sinking into a porch chair, "but neither Ward nor Sawyer would sign, even though they both want to stay here. Jim Ward has given up. He says it's no use to try to go against the government, and Emmet Sawyer told me he's never signed his name to anything, and he's not going to start now."

Hearing the note of resignation in his voice, Carrie frowned. "Maybe you'll have better luck tomorrow night, Grandpa," she said. "You haven't taken your petition to any of the neighbors below us. Or to any of the people east of the ridge. You could drive over there and talk to them, too."

"If I can't convince my own neighbors to sign, what kind of luck would I have with people who don't know me?" Grandpa asked.

Carrie hated to hear him sound so discouraged. "Maybe they'd sign if there were already lots of signatures on it. Sam Burns is sure to sign, and—"

"Mr. Burns," Grandma corrected automatically.

"I'll talk to the neighbors below us," Grandpa said, "but not tomorrow. I need to figure out a better way to approach people, a way that will make them want to sign."

Carrie drew a deep breath. For a minute she'd been afraid Grandpa was going to give up, but she should have known better than that.

* * *

The next evening, after dark, Sam Burns came slowly up the road and through the gate. He climbed the stairs to the porch and lowered himself into a chair. He didn't seem to notice Carrie sitting quietly on the porch swing.

"I've come to tell you something, Claude," he said, "and you're not going to like what I'm about to say."

"Well, if it's something I need to hear, you'd better go ahead and say it."

"Annie and I have decided not to fight this park thing," Sam began. "We're going to use the money from the state to buy a little place near our daughter, just outside Harrisonburg."

Carrie waited tensely to hear how Grandpa would respond. "I'm surprised to hear you're willing to give up your home like this," he said quietly.

Sam leaned forward. "You've got to remember, Claude, I'm a lot older than you are. Keeping up the place is getting to be too much for me."

Grandpa drummed his fingers on the arm of his chair. "Well," he said at last, "of all the people around here that are giving up, you're the only one with a good reason. Hugh Edwards and Jim Ward are cowed by the thought of going against the government," he said scornfully. "I guess they don't remember that in America the government's supposed to be 'of the people, by the people, and for the people.' But I believe those words, Sam," Grandpa continued. "And I believe citizens have the right to appeal to the government—and that when they do, they'll be treated fairly."

Carrie had been almost holding her breath during Grandpa's speech, and now she relaxed. Of course the government would treat them fairly!

"I know how strongly you feel about this thing, Claude," Sam said, "and I think you should go ahead and fight it as long as you can. But you'd better not count on getting much support from the other landowners along the road here." He paused for a moment, then went on. "The Landons are selling, too. They don't have roots here, you know. And when Annie was at the post office this morning, Mrs. Benton told her they've started looking for a place near Luray." He paused again and then added, "Old Mrs. Sly is going to move in with her son's family."

Grandpa sighed. "Well, you were right about one thing, Sam. I don't like what you came to tell me. But if everybody's already made plans to leave, I'd rather know it now than find out when I stopped by with my petition. I guess I'm going to have to give up on that idea and fight this alone."

In the darkness, Carrie couldn't see Grandpa's face. But she could tell by his voice how disappointed he was, and her heart ached for him. At first he'd hoped to save the homes of all the people in the mountains. Then he'd thought that at least the homes along the road would be spared. And tonight he'd learned that he'd have to fight alone.

She felt a surge of hope: Wouldn't it be easier to get the government to agree to spare just one place?

7

Writing to Mama was harder than ever this year, Carrie thought as she sat at the kitchen table with her pencil and paper Saturday morning. She didn't want to worry Mama by mentioning the park business, but there wasn't much else going on. Carrie looked critically at the border she'd doodled around the top sheet of her tablet and decided she could still use the paper for her letter. Maybe the border would make it less obvious that she didn't have much to say.

Dear Mama, she wrote, *I got your letters—sorry I waited so long to answer them. Hope you and Daddy are fine. We all are.* That part was easy enough. *Aunt Rose's family came for Sunday dinner right after I got here, and it was fun.* What else had happened? she wondered. Besides the park business, that is. *We went up on the ridge to visit some friends of Grandpa's last Sunday.* That was safe. Better not say Grandpa wrote a letter to the editor, or Mama would want to know what it was about. She needed just a couple more lines. *Sam and Annie Burns came up the other evening and had some of the pie Grandma and I baked. I'm helping a lot with the baking this year, and Grandma pays me half of what she makes from pie sales.*

Should she have told Mama about being paid? Probably not. She might object. Carefully, Carrie erased part of the last line and wrote a new ending that said, *and sometimes I work in the lunchroom, too.* It wouldn't hurt for Mama to know what she could do if somebody gave her the chance. Carrie read over what she'd written and changed "Sam and Annie" to "Mr. and Mrs.," trying to even out the spacing. Then she added, *Love, Carrie*, and began to address the envelope.

She was more than halfway to the post office when a movement a short distance ahead caught her eye—the lower limbs of the cherry tree in Mrs. Sly's yard were swaying strangely. Carrie's steps slowed as she tried to figure out what was going on. And then she saw a boy drop to the ground. It was Frank Benton, stealing the old woman's cherries. But he was supposed to be working on his uncle's farm this summer!

Frank dusted off his hands and glanced furtively around. When he spotted Carrie he gave a start, and then a grin spread slowly across his face. An evil grin, Carrie thought as her heart began to pound.

"Hey!" he called. "Got any petitions for me to sign?"

Carrie didn't know what to say—or what to do. If she walked toward the post office, there would be no way to avoid Frank, since his mother was postmistress and the small building was on his family's property. But if she turned toward home, he'd follow along and taunt her about Grandpa's petition and anything else he could think of.

"I just asked you something! Ain't you gonna answer me?" Frank called, walking toward her.

Stuffing the letter in her pocket, Carrie turned around and started uphill as fast as she could go without actually running. There was only one thing she could do.

"How come you're in such a hurry?" Frank yelled.

Carrie didn't have to look back to know he was following her. Thank goodness the Burns's gate was only a few yards ahead. She slipped through it and hurried up the walk. Pounding on the screen door, she willed Annie to come, and with great relief, she heard slow footsteps approaching.

"Why, hello, dear," Annie Burns said, smiling as she opened the door for Carrie. And then she saw Frank standing by the gate. "Are you coming in, too, Frankie?" she called.

Frank shook his head and ambled off, and Carrie wished she had the nerve to call, "Goodbye, *Frankie.*"

"I guess he's home because today's his mama's birthday," Annie said. "Now come to the kitchen and have a glass of lemonade with me." As she filled the glasses she said, "I'm surprised you aren't visiting with your little girlfriends this morning."

Before she knew it, Carrie found herself telling about Grandpa's politicking and how she hadn't seen Kate and Luanne since the night he'd made their father so angry.

"Well, everybody around here knows Claude Griffin is right outspoken. Some people just accept that about him, and others respect him for it. So I wouldn't worry, if I were you—I'd go right on up there and play with the Edwards girls instead of that awful Frankie Benton."

She'd go that very afternoon, Carrie decided. But she wished she hadn't told Annie what Grandpa had said to Mr. Edwards. Somehow it didn't seem quite right; if Mama knew, she'd call it "airing your dirty linen in public."

After she said good-bye to Annie Burns, Carrie turned uphill toward home. She'd mail Mama's letter on Monday, after Frank Benton had gone back to the valley. She was glad Annie hadn't guessed she'd stopped by just to get away from him. Only Amanda knew she was afraid of Frank—so afraid she'd hide behind an old lady's skirts to escape his taunts. "Someday I'll stand up to him," Carrie muttered. "And then he'll be sorry."

After the dishes were done that noon, Carrie told Grandma she was going to visit Kate and Luanne.

"Good," Grandma said. "You've waited long enough to let the dust settle but not so long that you'll feel strange together."

"What will I do if they don't want me to stay?"

"You'll come on home. But you have to find out how things stand between you."

A few minutes later, Carrie was walking up the road, stepping off into the tall grass beside the pavement occasionally when a car passed by. She waved to Mrs. Ward, who was shelling peas on her front porch, and hoped the whole Edwards family wouldn't be sitting outside when she arrived.

When Carrie rounded the next curve, her spirits rose—the girls were alone in their front yard. She grinned when she saw they had looped a long rope around a tree and were trying to jump Double Dutch with just one "ender." Sure now that they'd be glad to see her, she called to them.

They looked toward her and then at each other, and Carrie stopped short, one hand on the gate. Luanne glanced quickly over her shoulder and then started toward Carrie, but Kate grabbed her arm. "Do you want to get us a beating?" she cried.

Luanne shook her off. "You go on out back and make sure Tommy Tattle Tale don't come snooping around here while I'm talking to Carrie."

Carrie already knew what her friend was going to say, so she said it first. "Your father doesn't want me to come here."

Luanne nodded. "And he won't let us go to your house, either. We're not even supposed to speak to you."

Both girls gave a start when they heard Kate shriek, "You come back here, Tommy!"

Luanne dashed toward the house and Carrie hurried away. She didn't slow down until she'd rounded the first curve. Then, holding her head high, she breathed deeply, determined not to cry. She wasn't going to walk along the road with tears rolling down her cheeks the way she used to whenever Frank Benton teased her mercilessly.

The thought of Frank reminded her of how she'd fled from him that morning, and she scowled. This was one of the worst days of her life!

8

It rained on Sunday, a fine, misty drizzle that gave everything a soft, gray cast and muffled the sounds of the few cars that passed by. After dinner, Carrie and Amanda played checkers at the kitchen table while Grandma and Aunt Rose washed the dishes.

Carrie could hear the low rumble of the men's voices in the parlor and thuds and shouts from the front porch, where Clarence and Benjamin were racing back and forth. She and Amanda used to do that. Wistfully, Carrie remembered the satisfying feeling of her bare feet pounding on the boards as she and her cousin ran the length of the porch, shrieking with laughter.

"Ooh, I can jump your king!" Amanda squealed.

Carrie wished she'd been concentrating on the game instead of woolgathering. She made her move and settled back in her chair to plan her next turn. But Amanda took so long that Carrie's attention wandered again, and she found herself listening to the women's conversation. They were talking about the new park.

"What will happen if Dad can't convince them to change the boundary?" asked Aunt Rose.

"We'll lose the place, that's what will happen," Grandma answered shortly.

"I know that, Mama," Aunt Rose said patiently. "What I mean is, what will you and Dad do then?"

Shaken, Carrie watched Grandma turn to face her daughter.

"I don't know yet, Rose," she said.

"Haven't the two of you talked about it?"

Grandma plunged her hands into the dishpan. "All your father talks about is how he's going to fight this thing. He hasn't even considered the possibility that he might lose."

"But he's got to face that possibility—that *probability*!" Rose exclaimed. "You've got to see that he faces it, Mama."

Carrie was shocked. Aunt Rose thought Grandpa was going to lose!

"When you're as old as I am," Grandma said, rinsing out a glass, "then you can start telling me what I've got to do." When Aunt Rose didn't answer, Grandma went on. "A man needs to know his wife believes in him."

"Believes in him to do the impossible?" countered Rose.

"It's not impossible! It's not!" Carrie burst out. "Grandpa said he'd save this place, and he will!"

Grandma turned around. "Why, you girls were so quiet I'd forgotten you were here."

"Grandma, you don't think it's impossible, do you?" Carrie asked.

"Of course I don't," Grandma said briskly. "Now you girls go on with your game. Rose, I have something to show you upstairs."

The women dried their hands and left the kitchen, and Carrie heard Aunt Rose say, "I still think you have to face the fact that you'll probably have to leave here."

And Grandma replied, "I can face that fact, Rose, but I can't—"

The rest of her sentence was lost as they started upstairs. Carrie felt betrayed. Something to show her upstairs, indeed!

"It's your turn, Carrie," Amanda prompted.

"This is a stupid game!" Carrie said angrily. "I don't feel like playing anymore."

"Then we'll do something else," Amanda said. She swept the checkers together and began to put them in the box. "I guess you're not having a very good summer, with Grandma and Grandpa so worried about losing this place," she said, folding the checkerboard. "Do you wish you'd stayed in the city?"

Carrie was shocked at the question. "Of course not! I always come here—I'll never spend the summer anywhere else!"

Her words seemed to hang in the air between them. Finally, Amanda broke the silence. "Poor Carrie," she said, her brown eyes soft with sympathy. "Maybe you can spend the whole summer with us next year instead of just a week."

Carrie felt a rush of conflicting emotions. "You think Grandma and Grandpa are going to have to leave here," she said accusingly.

"Don't you? Really deep down?" Amanda asked.

"Of course I don't!" Carrie was close to tears. "Grandpa's going to get the government to change the park boundaries."

Amanda frowned. "But Mama says—"

"What does your mother know about anything?" Carrie interrupted. "Grandpa said he's going to stay here, and he will."

Quietly Amanda said, "I don't like it when you talk rudely about my mother, Carrie."

"I—I'm sorry, Amanda," Carrie said, looking at her cousin with new respect. Why couldn't *she* have stood up for Grandpa like that when Frank Benton taunted her about the petition? She should have said, "My grandfather has a petition, but it's just for grown-ups. Kids like you can't sign it." That would have shut him up.

"Why don't we play dominoes for a while," Amanda suggested.

Carrie quickly agreed. "Can you get them out of my room? I don't want to go upstairs right now." While her cousin was gone, Carrie went to the sink and filled a glass with water, hoping a cold drink would help her gain control of her feelings. She was glad Amanda never held a grudge. Maybe that was what made her so easy to be with—you didn't always have to watch what you said. If only Mama could be like that, too, Carrie thought wistfully.

After Aunt Rose's family left, Carrie went up to her room and shut the door. She lay on her stomach on the bed and waited, a *National Geographic* open in front of her. At last she heard Grandma coming up the stairs. Grandma stopped outside the closed door, just as Carrie had known she would.

"Carrie, are you all right?"

"Yes."

"May I come in?"

"If you want to." Carrie made her voice sound as toneless as she could. She didn't look up when Grandma came into the room and sat on the bed beside her.

"All right, Carrie. What is it?"

Carrie sat up, and the words came tumbling out. "I'm not some little kid like Clarence or Benjamin, you know. I'm old enough to know the truth about what's going on!" Her voice trembled with hurt and anger.

"You do know the truth about what's going on, Carrie."

Carrie looked at her uncertainly. "Then what did you tell Aunt Rose when you took her upstairs 'to show her something'?"

"Listen to me, Carrie. You know as much as any of us do. The government wants to take our land, and we want to keep it. Grandpa is doing all he can to try to keep it. He may succeed and he may not. Those are the facts, and it's your right to know them. But it's my right to talk to anyone I choose about those facts."

"Go on and say the rest of it," Carrie said coldly.

Grandma looked puzzled. "The rest of it?"

"Go ahead and say it's your right to talk anywhere you choose."

Grandma smoothed a wrinkle in the quilt before she answered. "You know, Carrie, you do have a habit of listening to grown-ups' conversations. Listening and interrupting."

Carrie was crushed. "But how else can I find out what's going on?" she whispered.

"Well," said Grandma, "you could wait to be told."

"Wait to be told!" Carrie's voice rose. "I'd wait forever! Nobody ever tells me anything!"

Grandma sighed. "You know that isn't true, Carrie. But there are some things you don't need to know. Things you don't need to worry about."

"You sound just like Mama!" Carrie said in disgust. "There's no need to worry, dear," she mimicked. "Everything will be all right."

"Now, don't you mock your mama," Grandma said sternly. "She's doing what she thinks is best for you."

"But what's best for me is to know what's happening even if I do worry!"

After a moment Grandma said, "I think your Mama decided to raise you differently than she was raised. I think she's trying to give you a childhood that's free of work and worry."

So that was why Mama never let her help, and why Mama and Daddy sometimes stopped talking when she came into the room, Carrie realized. "I'd rather work and worry along with the rest of the family, like I do here," she said at last.

"Have you ever told your mama that?" Grandma asked.

"Of course not!"

"Well, maybe you ought to."

Carrie looked at Grandma in surprise. "I couldn't do that!"

"I don't see why not. You certainly don't seem to have any trouble telling me how you feel."

"That—that's different," Carrie said, not sure how to explain that at home nobody ever talked about feelings. And nobody showed their feelings much, either. Somehow, though, it seemed safe to do that here. "I'm sorry I shut the door, Grandma," she said quietly. "And that I talked back to you."

"And I'm sorry you felt left out when I went upstairs to talk to Rose. Now give me a big hug," Grandma said, reaching out to her, "and then we'll go downstairs and fix some cocoa."

9

Carrie knotted a handful of change in the corner of her handkerchief and clattered down the stairs, wearing shoes for almost the first time since she'd arrived more than two weeks before.

Grandpa pulled out his pocket watch. "We ought to be there in plenty of time for the Fourth of July festivities," he said.

The ride to Luray seemed to take forever, but at last they turned into the fairgrounds and Grandpa carefully parked the car against the fence. Carrie's eyes searched the crowd until she spotted Uncle George, with Benjamin riding on his shoulders.

"I'll be with Amanda," Carrie told her grandparents, setting off to meet her cousin.

"Can I go now, Mama?" Amanda asked when Carrie came up.

And Clarence chimed in, "And me and Ben, too?"

"Run along, all of you," Aunt Rose said. "And Amanda, you keep an eye on your brothers."

Carrie took Benjamin's hand, but Clarence walked a few steps ahead of the girls as they started toward the sunny field where the day's events were about to begin. On the way, Carrie saw Kate and Luanne picnicking under a tree with their family, and without thinking, she waved to them. The girls just looked down at their plates, but Tommy stuck out his tongue. Carrie's face flushed with embarrassment and anger. She felt a bit better, though, when she saw Moses give his little brother's arm a hard punch—and when she realized her cousins hadn't noticed anything.

"That's Sheriff Holmes," Amanda said, pointing to a man in uniform who was staking down a rope to form the starting line. "Isn't he handsome?" Turning to her brothers she said, "You two better go on up there. They always have the little kids' races first."

The boys ran toward the group of youngsters, where a deputy was handing out burlap sacks. The sheriff called out, "All right, everybody. Line up at the rope for the sack race." He bent to help Benjamin step into his sack and rolled the top down for him to hold on to. "There you are, sonny," he said. Then he shouted, "On your mark! Get set! Go!"

Carrie and Amanda cheered when Clarence began to pull ahead of the others, then groaned as Benjamin tripped over his sack and went sprawling. In a few quick strides, Sheriff Holmes reached him and set him on his feet again, saying, "Pull up on the top of that sacking and it won't tangle 'round your feet."

"C'mon, Benjamin! You can do it!" Carrie shouted as her little cousin started off again.

Some of the adults stood at the end of the course, cheering on their favorites. Carrie saw Clarence cross the finish line in second place and proudly accept a handshake from his father and grandfather. And finally, bringing up the rear, little Benjamin gave one last hop and then rolled across the line.

"Hurray for Benjamin!" Carrie shouted.

The sheriff turned to her and smiled. "That's a game little kid. Is he your brother?"

"He's my cousin," Carrie answered shyly. .

"He's *my* brother, Sheriff," said Amanda. "And the boy who came in second is my brother, too."

"Well," said the sheriff, "let's see if you can do as well as they did." And he called to the waiting group, "All right, the sack race for the rest of you kids is next."

"Come on, Carrie," said Amanda, starting forward.

A group of older boys and girls crowded around the deputy to get their sacks, and Carrie caught her breath when she saw Frank Benton shoving his way to the front. There was no mistaking his insolent expression, even at this distance, and Carrie felt her stomach start to knot up. "I don't think I'll race this year, Amanda," she said, hanging back.

"Don't be silly," said Amanda, grabbing her arm. "Come on!"

Carrie pulled away. "You go ahead. I'll wait for you."

But as she watched the contestants climbing into their sacks, Carrie could almost smell the earthy scent of the burlap and feel its scratchiness against her bare legs. Why was she letting Frank Benton keep her out of the race? If he bothered her, she'd just say, "Stop that, *Frankie!*" Grinning at the thought, she started toward the group, hoping there'd be a sack left. But then Sheriff Holmes called out, "On your mark!"

Disappointed, Carrie turned and walked slowly toward a nearby maple. From its shade, she watched Amanda bobbing up and down with each of her quick little hops and saw

Frank making long, ungainly leaps. He was the fourth to cross the finish line and was obviously furious that he hadn't won. Scornfully, Carrie followed him with her eyes as he threw his sack on the grass and stalked away. "I shouldn't have let him scare me off," she muttered.

Amanda was among the last to cross the finish line. She climbed out of her sack and handed it to a deputy before she ran over to Carrie. "That was fun!" she said, panting. "Don't you wish you'd raced, too?" She was red and sweaty, and her braids were coming undone.

"Turn around," Carrie said, ignoring her question, "and I'll fix your hair for you." She was tying the ribbon around the second braid when the deputy handed Amanda a wide strip of cloth torn from a sheet.

Amanda thrust it at her. "Hurry, Carrie! We don't want to miss the three-legged race!"

Carrie grabbed the cloth. She put her left leg against Amanda's right and stooped over to tie them together, winding the long cloth strip around and around, pulling it snug, but not too tight. She straightened up just as the line of younger children lurched and hobbled forward. Some distance away, Frank Benton was berating his red-haired partner for tying their legs too loosely, and Carrie wondered if he was mean to everybody.

When their age group was called, Carrie and Amanda placed their tied-together legs just behind the starting line and slipped their arms around each other's waists. Across the way Grandpa shouted, "C'mon, girls!"

Carrie looked around and saw to her dismay that all the other racers were boys. She glanced up at Sheriff Holmes, and he grinned and winked. Tightening her arm around her cousin's waist, she said determinedly, "Let's show these boys, Amanda!"

Before Amanda could reply, the sheriff called out, "On your mark!" The girls leaned slightly forward. "Get set!" They shifted their weight to their forward legs. "Go!" They moved off as smoothly as if they were a single person. But as the long-legged boys on either side strode forward, Carrie feared that she and Amanda would soon be left behind. And to make things worse, a high-pitched voice yelled from the sidelines, "Nyah, nyah! Girls can't—"

From the corner of her eye, Carrie saw Moses Edwards clap his hand over his little brother's mouth. "Come on, Carrie!" he shouted. "You can do it!"

One of the boys on Carrie and Amanda's left slowed slightly as he turned to see who was cheering for the girls, and his partner stumbled forward. The last glimpse Carrie had of them, they were struggling to their feet. She and Amanda had almost caught up to the boys on their right when one of the pair looked back just as the other lengthened his stride. A moment later, both were on the ground.

The girls glided forward almost effortlessly, their movements perfectly synchronized, steadily gaining on the other racers. They were pulling ahead of the pack! Carrie could feel her heart pounding with excitement. Now only the two boys on the far side of the course were ahead of them, advancing rapidly with awkward, jerky movements. Wasn't one of them—?

"We'll be second!" Amanda gasped.

A roar went up from the crowd as the larger boy pitched forward onto the grass, pulling his partner down with him. "We'll be *first!*" Carrie cried, and to the sound of wild cheering, they sailed across the finish line just seconds before Frank Benton—it *was* Frank!—and his red-haired partner scrambled across it on their hands and knees.

Grandpa and Uncle George hugged the girls, and Clarence and Benjamin jumped up and down. An old farmer came up to them and said, "Girlies, that was the purtiest race I ever seen!"

Carrie was a little embarrassed by all the attention, but Amanda seemed to enjoy it. Finally she turned to Carrie and said, "Can you believe we were first? Isn't it wonderful?"

"It sure is," Carrie agreed. Imagine beating Frank Benton!

"I never thought we'd beat those last two boys," Amanda went on, "and neither did they. Did you see the look on the bigger one's face?"

"That was Frank Benton," Carrie whispered, glancing around, but Frank and his partner had already slunk away.

Amanda's eyes lit up. "The mean kid who's always bothering you? Well, I guess we showed him!"

"I guess so," Carrie said, bending down to untie the cloth strip that still bound her leg to Amanda's. But even though she and Amanda had beaten him in the race, Carrie knew she really hadn't shown him anything. "What are we going to do next?" she asked, straightening up.

"We want to go to the pie eating contest," said Clarence.

"Can we, Carrie? Can we?" begged Benjamin, tugging at her skirt.

Carrie looked down at their eager faces and her heart fell. After all the baking she'd been doing, she didn't want to even think about pies today! "How 'bout if I treat you to some ice cream instead?"

She was relieved at their instant agreement, and they set off toward the ice-cream stand. When she heard someone call her name, Carrie looked back and saw Moses Edwards grin and raise his clasped hands above his head. Pleased, she waved to him. Was he just trying to make up for his little brother's rudeness, or—

"Who's that?" Amanda asked. "He's cute!"

"That's Moses Edwards. You know, Kate and Luanne's brother."

Before Amanda could respond, Clarence began to chant, "Carrie's got a boyfriend! Carrie's got a boyfriend!"

"Do you want to meet my boyfriend, Clarence? We can go talk to him instead of getting ice cream," Carrie said. That shut him up fast, she thought with satisfaction, wishing she could deal with Frank Benton that easily.

There was a line at the ice-cream stand, and while Amanda and the boys were deciding which flavor they wanted, the words of a conversation behind her caught Carrie's ear.

". . . letter to the editor in last week's paper? It was from the man who runs the store out where the road crosses the mountain—don't recall his name."

"That would be Claude Griffin. What did he have to say?"

The other man laughed. "A lot of crazy ideas for how the people could keep the government from taking over their land. He even said that everybody up on the mountain should chip in so they could hire themselves a lawyer. Some people don't know when they're licked."

How dare he talk like that about Grandpa! Remembering how Amanda had stood up for her mother, Carrie turned to confront the speaker, a portly, ruddy-faced man whose bald head glistened with sweat, and when he caught her eye, he grinned and winked.

Flustered, Carrie looked away. All she'd needed to do was say, "That's my grandfather you're talking about, and I don't like what you're saying." But could she do it? No.

And then she felt Benjamin tugging at her skirt again. "We're next, Carrie, and I want chocolate."

She bought four chocolate cones and they started off, licking the ice cream as they went. But Carrie hardly tasted hers. She kept hearing the words "crazy ideas . . . crazy ideas . . . some people don't know when they're licked . . . they're licked . . . they're licked . . . ."

"Come on, Carrie," Amanda said, nudging her. "It's almost time for the horseshoe match, and we have to wish Daddy and Grandpa good luck. I'll race you!"

Carrie didn't feel much like racing, but she didn't want to spoil Amanda's fun. So the girls set off, with Clarence at their heels and Benjamin tagging along behind. Grandpa and Uncle George were standing with some other men, so Carrie stopped a little distance away, but Amanda ran right up to them and turned to give Carrie a triumphant look. Carrie hardly noticed. Grandpa was talking about the park, and she wanted to hear what he was saying.

"We're right on the main road, so all they'd have to do is draw the boundary back two or three hundred yards to exclude my acreage, and—"

"But what about the property owner beyond you? And the one beyond him?" someone interrupted. "If they make an exception for you, wouldn't they have to make one for everybody that asked?"

Carrie frowned. What the man said made sense. But Grandpa's reply set her mind at ease.

"If they move the boundary back from the road, it would spare the homes of nearly all the people that want to stay. Most of the folks further up on the ridge are willing to go," Grandpa answered.

"That ain't so," protested a bearded man in overalls. "Not a single soul in my hollow wants to leave."

"My kin on Catlett Mountain don't want to, either," agreed a younger man who had been listening quietly. "They've got a good life there."

"All the folks that wanted to go, they already sold out. Us that's still there, we want to stay," declared the bearded man.

"Well, then," Grandpa began enthusiastically, "you should all join together and oppose the unconstitutional seizure of your property. Why, if enough—"

But he was interrupted by a young man in a red plaid shirt. "Listen to him, now. Don't he sound just like that feller who wrote in to the paper? Next he'll be suggestin' all that riffraff up on the ridge hire theirselves a lawyer!"

There was an angry murmuring in the crowd. Grandpa rested his hand on the bearded mountaineer's arm and took a step toward the younger man, and suddenly Carrie was apprehensive.

Uncle George cleared his throat and said loudly, "Looks like they're ready to start the match. We'd better take our places."

The men began to scatter, and a feeling of relief swept over Carrie. Uncle George never had much to say, but he could speak up when it counted! Carrie walked over to where Grandpa stood, clenching and unclenching his fists, his face pale beneath his summer tan.

"Good luck in the horseshoe match, Grandpa," she said.

He managed a smile, but his eyes were still hard with anger. "Thanks, Carrie," he said. "I need all the luck I can get."

"What do you want to do next?" Amanda asked.

"Let's play bingo," Carrie suggested. She was tired, and her face and arms felt hot from standing in the sun so long. It would be good to sit under the canopy and do nothing more than listen to the caller and place kernels of corn over numbers on a bingo card.

"You youngsters be sure to meet us in time for the speeches," Grandpa called after them.

"We never had to listen to the speeches before," Carrie protested. "Why do we have to this year?"

Grandpa looked stern. "I want you to understand what this celebration is about. What the Declaration of Independence means to all of us today."

"But I do understand, Grandpa. We studied it at school, and I practically know it by heart! It means freedom from government tyranny. It means the right to have a say in what the government decides, and—" Carrie stopped suddenly.

"That's exactly what it does mean," Grandpa said firmly. "And it's important for you to hear about it, over and over, so you don't forget it. Especially now."

Carrie nodded soberly. "We'll be there, Grandpa," she said.

As they started off, Clarence looked up at Carrie and asked, "Do you really know the Declaration of Independence by heart?"

"Of course I do. Want to hear it?"

"Not right now," Clarence said, edging away.

But Carrie grabbed him by the arm. "Oh, yes, you do." Still holding onto Clarence, she stood with her right hand over her heart, as if she were saluting the flag, and recited: "Every American has the right to own land, and no one has to give up their land just because somebody else wants it, even if that somebody else is the government."

Clarence pulled away from her. "You're foolin' us, Carrie. It doesn't say that at all."

"Did you ever read it?"

Clarence shook his head.

"Then how do you know it doesn't say that?"

" 'Cause the government *is* going to take Grandpa's land! Daddy says so."

Amanda made a dive for her brother, shrieking, "I told you not to say that in front of Carrie!"

Clarence turned and ran, with Amanda in hot pursuit and little Benjamin following along behind, shouting, "Catch 'im, Manda! Catch 'im!"

Stunned, Carrie stood looking after them.

10

Carrie's heart leaped when she saw Kate and Luanne coming toward the gate. Leaving her book on the porch swing, she ran to meet them, calling, "Did your father change his mind?" Kate shook her head. "Mama sent us to the store for coffee."

"But she said she wouldn't need us till time to help with supper, so she don't mind if we visit a while," Luanne added.

"What about Tommy?" Carrie asked apprehensively.

Luanne grinned. "We don't have to worry about him this afternoon—Mama made Moses take him along when he went fishing."

"Then come on over to the lunchroom after Grandpa grinds your coffee," Carrie said. "I'll get us some pop out of the icebox."

A few minutes later, the girls were sitting around one of the tables with their cold drinks. "We're sorry about ignoring you on the Fourth," Kate said, "but if we'd waved back, our father probably would have taken us all straight home."

"That's okay," said Carrie, thinking how awful it must be to have a father like Mr. Edwards.

"Want to play 'I Doubt It?' We brought our cards." Luanne reached into her pocket and pulled out the deck.

The girls were on their third game when the door to the lunchroom opened and a shrill voice said, "Aha! I thought so—and I'm gonna tell, too!" There stood Tommy, gleefully pointing at his sisters. Both girls froze, and Tommy backed out the door, singsonging, "You're gonna get it, you're gonna get it, you're gonna . . ."

"I guess we should have played in the house," Carrie said when his words faded away.

Kate just stared at the table, but Luanne shook her head. "It wouldn't have made no difference. If he thought we were here, he'd have hung around till he saw us leave. I guess we shouldn't have stayed, but I'm glad we did."

"We'd better go now," Kate said, her voice trembling.

"Might as well be hanged for a sheep as a lamb," Luanne said, picking up her cards. "At least that's what Mama always says."

But the afternoon was spoiled, and after one more game the girls went home, carrying their bag of coffee. Kate's feet dragged and her shoulders slumped, but Luanne carried herself proudly. Carrie wondered how her friend could face certain punishment so bravely. She was putting the empty pop bottles in the case when the lunchroom door opened and a tired-looking couple with a fussy toddler came in.

Grandma was right on their heels. "Oh, I didn't know you were over here, Carrie," she said. "Go ahead and take their order while I fix a fresh pot of coffee."

After the young family had gone, Carrie swept up the

crumbs the baby had made, and Grandma washed his sticky handprints off the oilcloth table cover. "I saw the Edwards girls going up the road as I came over. Did they stay for a while?" she asked.

Carrie told her about the visit and how Tommy had burst in on them. "Why does he always want to get Kate and Luanne in trouble?" she asked.

Grandma sighed. "That little boy does everything he can to get on the good side of his father, including seeing to it that nobody disobeys him when he's not there. I think it's his way of protecting himself from Hugh Edwards' bad temper."

That made sense, Carrie thought, but somebody ought to protect Kate and Luanne from Tommy! "Well, I guess I'd better go down to the post office," she said, putting away her broom.

Grandma looked up when Carrie came back to the lunchroom with a letter. "Is that from your mama?" she asked.

"Yes, and it's for you this time," Carrie answered, handing the letter to her grandmother.

Grandma sat down at one of the tables to read it. "Your mama says you haven't written home yet this summer," she said, looking up.

"I wrote her a letter Saturday, but I didn't mail it till Monday," Carrie said guiltily, remembering how she'd fled from Frank. She slipped into the chair across from Grandma. "I know I shouldn't have waited so long, but there's nothing much to write about this year."

"Nothing much to write about! There's more going on around here this summer than any other time I can remember!"

"Yes, but I can't tell Mama about the park."

Grandma stared at her. "I don't see why not!"

"It would just worry her."

"Wait a minute, now. I distinctly remember you complaining that your mama never tells you anything, and now you're keeping this from her." When Carrie didn't answer, Grandma added, "She already knows about the park business, anyway—I mentioned it in my last letter."

"And now I'll bet she's written back to tell you not to worry, that everything's going to be all right!" Carrie was surprised at her sudden feeling of anger toward her mother.

Grandma folded the letter and slipped it back into the envelope. "She's sure it will all work out for the best," she said after a moment. "I wish I could be sure of that. All I know is that we'll manage, one way or another, however it works out."

Before Carrie could respond, the screen door opened and a stout woman in a dark blue dress came into the lunchroom.

"Why, Molly Hughes! It's been a right long time since I've seen you!" Grandma exclaimed, tucking the letter into her apron pocket. "You remember my granddaughter, Carrie, don't you? She'll bring us some iced tea and a piece of custard pie while we visit."

Molly Hughes pulled out a chair and carefully settled herself into it. Then she reached down and slipped off her shoes. "Oh, my feet!" she moaned. "What a day this has been!"

"You're all dressed up for such a hot afternoon," Grandma observed.

"Henry and I just been to a funeral," the woman answered. "Thought we'd stop in on our way home, since we was passing by."

"I'm glad you did," said Grandma as Carrie brought their refreshments and then tactfully returned to her place behind the counter. "I hadn't heard of any deaths. Whose funeral was it?" Grandma asked.

"Henry's old uncle. His father's brother. He lived way up on the ridge—took us forever to get there on those bad roads, and then we had to walk quite a way from the house to the graveyard. No wonder my feet hurt!"

"Had the old man been sick long?" Grandma asked sympathetically.

Mrs. Hughes shook her head and leaned forward to whisper something to Grandma. Carrie couldn't hear what she said, but she saw Grandma's hand fly to her face in shock.

Mrs. Hughes leaned back in her chair again. "His son, Henry's first cousin, found him. Hanging from a rafter in the barn."

Carrie could hardly believe her ears!

"Do they have any idea why he did it?" asked Grandma.

The woman nodded. "They know why he did it, all right. He didn't want to leave his place, and they was about to take it for that park. He told everybody that he'd lived all his life there and he planned to die there, too. But his son thought that was just a manner of speaking. Nobody thought he was going to—was going to do what he did." Her plump hands twisted her lace-trimmed handkerchief.

Grandma looked out the window. "I guess it's hard for people that old to face up to change. My neighbor Lizzy Ward told me about an old woman who lived up in the mountains in the same log cabin she was born in. Every time anybody came to talk to her about leaving, she'd just sit there in her rocking chair and say, 'I've told you before and I'm telling you again. I'll not be taken out of here alive.' "

Carrie leaned across the counter, abandoning all pretense of not listening. Grandpa wasn't the only one refusing to leave his land!

"Well," Grandma continued, "finally Sheriff Holmes went and talked to her oldest son about it, and the next day all her children went up to see her. They tried and tried to get her to go and live in the valley with one of them. One of her sons even offered to build her a cabin on his farm. But she told them there was no need for that. 'You don't have to worry none. I'll not be taken out of here alive,' she said. And you know, she died in her bed that very night, just as though she'd willed it that way."

Carrie had been almost holding her breath during Grandma's story, and now she let it out all at once. That old woman had died rather than leave her home!

Grandma went on. "Her children buried her right there on her place, figuring that was what she'd have wanted."

They all gave a start as the screen door opened and

Henry Hughes came in. He was short and bald, and Carrie thought he looked uncomfortable in his good suit.

"I was sorry to hear about your uncle," Grandma said to him.

Henry Hughes shook his head. "That was a sad thing. They ought to let the old folks stay up there. They wouldn't do no harm to the park." Then, resting his hand on his wife's plump shoulder, he said, "We'd best be getting on home, Molly."

Carrie came out from behind the counter and joined Grandma at the table as soon as they left.

"I'm sorry you heard that story about Henry's old uncle," Grandma said, looking at Carrie with concern. "I can see it's upset you."

"Grandma," Carrie said in a quavering voice, "do you remember that first night I was here?"

"Not 'specially. I remember I was right glad to see you, though." She smiled at Carrie.

"But do you remember what Grandpa said that night?"

"He said a lot of things, Sunshine. What are you thinking about?"

"He was talking about this place, and he said he was born here and he intended to die here." Carrie bit the inside of her lower lip to keep it from trembling.

"Pull yourself together, now," Grandma said sternly. "Don't you know your grandpa any better than that? He's a fighter. We'll not be cutting him down from any barn rafters."

"Even if—if he loses the fight?" Asking this made Carrie feel like a traitor, but she had to know.

"If he loses, he'll know he put everything he had into it. He won't have to wonder whether things would've been different if he'd tried harder. He'll grieve awhile, but then he'll get on with his life." And Grandma added, very quietly, "And then I'll be able to get on with my own life, too."

Grandma had given up hope, Carrie realized in dismay. She didn't think they'd be able to keep the place. Maybe Grandpa really was fighting a losing battle, like Aunt Rose and Uncle George—and those men at the fairgrounds on the Fourth—said! A feeling of panic began to well up in Carrie, but she fought it down. No matter what anybody else thought, Grandpa was going to win.

Why was Sport barking? Carrie wondered, heading for the front door. When she saw Moses Edwards standing at the gate, her heart beat a little faster—he'd never come to visit her before! She hurried outside and quieted the dog. "Come on in," she said. "He won't bite you."

Moses shook his head. "I just came to give you a message from Kate and Luanne. From now on, if Mama needs something at the store, I'm supposed to get it, and Tommy's going to get the mail. The girls wanted you to know so you wouldn't be watching for them."

"Did your father—that is, are Kate and Luanne—" Carrie stopped, not knowing quite how to ask what she wanted to know. But Moses seemed to understand.

"They're fine. It was Mama he was mad at, for sending them to the store." His Adam's apple bobbed as he swallowed hard.

Carrie didn't want to think about what must have happened when Tommy told Mr. Edwards that Kate and Luanne had disobeyed him. "Well, he'd have been even madder if there hadn't been any coffee at suppertime, wouldn't he?" she asked.

"Yes, but he'd just bought coffee himself last week." Moses patted Sport, who had put his front paws on the top of the gate, and then looked at Carrie. "Some day I'm gonna drown that sorry kid."

He said it with such passion that she half believed him. "Well, tell Kate and Luanne—" She stopped again. What could she tell them?

"I'll just tell them you said hello," Moses said, giving Sport one last pat before he started home.

Carrie's eyes followed him as he headed up the road. If only Grandpa hadn't made Mr. Edwards so angry, she thought. He obviously was never going to relent and let Kate and Luanne visit, and thanks to Tommy Tattle Tale, there was no chance her friends would disobey their father again. Not when it meant his anger would be turned on their mother.

Wondering if she'd ever see Moses when his mother sent him to the store, she set off for the post office.

"We both got letters today, Grandma," Carrie announced, coming into the lunchroom a short time later. "Yours is from somebody in Maryland."

They sat down at one of the tables to read. It was nice to get mail, Carrie thought as she tore open the envelope, but she didn't have to read her letter from home to know what it would say: Mama was busy, Daddy was working hard, they both missed her, and the weather was nice. Not a word about how stifling hot it was in their fourth floor apartment. Not a word about the old man next door who was so sick. He must not be any better; Mama would have mentioned if he were, just to have something to say.

And then Carrie realized that finding something to write about must be just as hard for her mother as it was for her, and she felt a little guilty for being so critical. The important thing, after all, was keeping in touch, not what was said, she thought as she began to read.

Dear Carrie,

I'm glad you're having a good summer. Your father and I miss you, but he's working very hard and I'm keeping busy here at home. The weather—

Carrie and Grandma both looked up when they heard a commotion on the store porch and then Grandpa's angry voice shouting, "If you're going to buy something, buy it! Otherwise, get off my property!"

And then a quieter voice said, "If you don't mind, I'll have a cup of coffee at the lunchroom before I go."

"Well, make sure you leave as soon as you finish it."

Carrie and Grandma were behind the counter by the time a tall man in city clothes stepped inside. He took off his hat and set it on a chair with his briefcase.

"Could I help you, sir?" asked Grandma.

"I'd like a ham sandwich and a cup of coffee, please," the man answered, sitting down at the counter. "Are you Mrs. Griffin?"

"Yes, I am," Grandma answered.

"I'm one of the state appraisers. My job is to make sure the Commonwealth of Virginia pays a fair price for farms that are inside the boundaries of the new Shenandoah National Park."

"We don't want to sell," Grandma said firmly.

"I got that impression from your husband. He ordered me off his property." The man sipped his coffee. "You have a nice place here, Mrs. Griffin. I can see why you don't want to leave."

"My husband hopes he can work things out so we can stay."

The man nodded. "For your sake, I hope so, too. But I don't think there's much chance." He finished his sandwich and wiped his hands on the napkin. "May I have another cup of coffee, please?" he asked, smiling at Carrie.

"Thank you, miss," he said when she brought it. Then he turned to Grandma. "I have to look over your property, ma'am."

"My husband—"

"Mrs. Griffin, the Commonwealth of Virginia wants to pay a fair price for land it's condemned for the park, but unless I can look at your buildings and see how much land you have in orchards and pasture, there's no way to judge what this place is worth."

Carrie held her breath and waited for Grandma's reply.

"My husband has ordered you off the property as soon as you're through in here, and he'll keep you off, too. He's always around—except when he goes to town early Thursday mornings."

The man hesitated a moment, then gave a brief nod. He finished his coffee and counted out some coins. "That was delicious, Mrs. Griffin," he said. "And you can rest assured that you'll get a fair price for this place if you do have to sell." He picked up his hat and briefcase and went out.

Carrie watched Grandma put the dishes in the dishpan and wipe the counter. When she glanced up and their eyes met, Carrie looked back accusingly. Grandma sighed and said, "Hope for the best and prepare for the worst. That's my motto. And I do have to prepare for the worst, Carrie. *Somebody* has to."

On Thursday morning Grandma minded the store while Grandpa drove to Luray to do his weekly errands. Carrie sat under one of the tall poplar trees in the front yard, idly petting Sport. When the official-looking black car slowed down to pull off the paved road, she jumped to her feet, and when the tall man stepped out of the car, she ran to the gate. But Sport blocked her way, barking and growling deep in his throat as the man approached. Carrie had to shut the dog in the toolshed before the appraiser could come into the yard.

"Grandma wants me to show you around. What do you want to see first?" she asked.

"Suppose we start with the farm buildings out back. You can answer some questions about the house while we're walking," he said, opening his long yellow tablet to a fresh page.

After he'd made notes about when the house was built and how many rooms it had, the appraiser paced off the dimensions of the outbuildings and jotted them down. He avoided the toolshed, where Sport was barking and pawing at the door, but he inspected the woodshed, the chicken house, the washhouse where Grandma kept her prized gasoline-fueled washing machine, the open-ended car shed, and even the long-abandoned barn. Then he looked at the garden and walked along the edge of the orchard, making more notes. Carrie watched his eyes sweep across the pasture where the neighbor's cattle grazed.

"That's our timberland on the far side of the pasture. Do you have to look at it, too?" she asked nervously.

The appraiser glanced at his watch. "I think I've seen all I need to, and you've given me enough information about the house. I'll leave as soon as I've spoken to your grandmother."

"You can't do that!" Carrie cried. The man looked at her in surprise, and Carrie's face burned with embarrassment. What must he think of her? "You see," she went on, "when—when my grandpa gets back, he—he might ask her if you've been around."

The appraiser's face cleared and he nodded. "I understand. She wants to be able to say she hasn't seen me." At the gate he turned to Carrie and said, "Don't forget to let your dog out. You'd have a hard time explaining why he was locked in the toolshed."

Carrie felt ashamed to be tricking Grandpa like this,

but how could she have refused to go along with Grandma's plan? How could she have said she wouldn't do her part to make sure they got a good price for the place if things went wrong? Preparing for the worst didn't mean she believed the worst was going to happen, after all.

The appraiser had been gone only a few minutes when Grandpa jerked the old Dodge to a stop outside the store and ran up the steps. Carrie heard him calling, "Sarah! Sarah, I just passed a state car on the road. Was that land appraiser here again?"

Standing just inside the lunchroom door, Carrie strained her ears to hear Grandma's reply: "I sure didn't see him, Claude," she said. "He knows you don't want him around, and I don't think he'll be coming here again."

All that morning Carrie worried about what to say in case Grandpa asked if she'd seen the appraiser. She couldn't lie to him, but she couldn't tell him the truth, either. A trickle of sweat ran down her face and she wiped it off with her arm. It was hot in the kitchen, and baking pies by herself wasn't any fun at all. She missed Kate and Luanne, too. It wasn't fair—this park business was ruining her summer!

Carrie almost wished she were back in the city, sharing secrets with the other girls in the neighborhood and going to the movies on Saturday afternoons. But she reminded herself that it was better to be here, sharing all this trouble with her grandparents, than to be at home, pretending everything was just fine. Besides, Grandpa needed her here because she was the only one who believed in him.

But Grandpa wouldn't think she believed in him if he

found out she'd showed the appraiser around. Sighing, Carrie picked up the potholders to lift her pies from the oven. When the back door opened and Grandpa called her name, she gave a guilty start and her hand brushed the oven rack.

Grandpa came into the kitchen and stopped short at the sight of her tears. "What's the matter, Carrie?" he asked.

"I burned my hand a little, that's all," she said, wiping her eyes.

Grandpa looked at the angry red mark. "It's not too bad, but it'll hurt awhile, anyway," he said. "I'll send your Grandma over to fix it for you."

Carrie's knees went weak with relief when the back door shut behind him. "At least it kept him from asking about the appraiser," she said aloud, looking at her hand.

To Carrie's surprise, Grandma broke off a piece of the spiky plant on her kitchen windowsill and squeezed its juice onto the burn. "Aloe vera is the best thing I know of for healing burns," Grandma said. "Now, go upstairs and lie down for a while. I'll bring your dinner up to you."

"Oh, I'll be fine, Grandma. It hardly hurts at all now."

Grandma gave her a meaningful look. "I think it would be a good idea, anyway," she said.

Carrie suddenly saw that Grandma, too, was worried about the questions Grandpa might have for her. "Oh, Grandma, what will I say if he asks me?" she cried.

"By suppertime he probably won't be thinking about that any more. Now go along, and don't worry. Remember, you did what had to be done. That's all anybody can do."

*   *   *

From her bedroom window, Carrie saw Sam Burns walk slowly up the road to the store that afternoon and then start toward home, empty-handed, a few minutes later. He must have come to tell Grandpa something, she thought, wondering what was so important it brought the old man out in the heat of the day.

At suppertime, she found out. Grandpa was jubilant when he announced that the park boundary had been redrawn to exclude a nearby hollow where there was a community with a church and school as well as a number of homes. "If they've spared that hollow, I'm sure we can save this place," he said confidently.

Carrie's spirits rose. Everything would work out. Already, Grandpa seemed more like himself than he had since all this park business began.

"How 'bout a little game of checkers, Sunshine?" he suggested. "Let's see if you remember that trick I taught you."

It was the best evening they'd had in weeks. Grandma made popcorn and lemonade and then joined them at the table with her mending. They laughed and joked together, just like old times, and Carrie played better than she ever had before.

12

Except for not seeing Kate and Luanne, the next week was almost like Carrie's other summers in the mountains. The park business seemed to be forgotten. The only time it was even mentioned was when Aunt Rose brought it up at Sunday dinner, much to Carrie's distress.

But on Thursday when Grandpa came home from town, everything changed. "Word's gotten 'round that a man from that hollow is pretty deeply involved in county politics," he announced at dinner. "That's how come they changed the boundary. Influence—political influence!" He banged his fist on the table and glared at Grandma and Carrie.

No one ate much for the rest of the meal, and when they heard a car stop in front of the store, Grandpa said, "Sarah, would you take care of my customers this afternoon? There's something I have to do." He left the table, and Grandma and Carrie stared after him for a moment before Grandma hurried out and Carrie began to put the leftovers away.

A few minutes later, Grandpa returned to the kitchen and sat down at the table. Carrie saw that he'd brought a pen and an ink bottle, a tablet of unlined paper, and an envelope. From the corner of her eye, she watched him tip the ink bottle to fill the little well on the side. Then he unscrewed the lid, dipped in his pen, and began to write.

Carrie worked slowly, washing each dish carefully and wiping it long after it was dry. She scrubbed the pots and pans longer than necessary, too, but when she finally left the kitchen, Grandpa was still writing.

Carrie had been sitting on the porch for a long time, petting Sport and wondering about the letter, when Grandpa came out and said, "I'm going down to the post office, Sunshine. Want to come along?"

She jumped up. This was her chance to find out about his mysterious letter! "I'll tell Grandma we're going," she said.

But as they walked along, instead of talking about what he'd written, Grandpa told her the name of every kind of roadside wildflower and identified every bird call. Carrie gritted her teeth. She wasn't interested in a nature lesson! She was glad when they reached the tiny post office.

"I need a stamp to mail this letter to Washington, D.C.," Grandpa said, counting out three pennies.

"Another letter to your daughter?" asked Mrs. Benton, smiling as she handed him the stamp.

"Nope, not this time," replied Grandpa.

"I know—you're writing to the president!" she joked.

"Thought I'd try the secretary of the interior first," said Grandpa, licking the stamp.

Carrie frowned. Who was that?

The postmistress chuckled and reached for the letter, but when she saw the address she became serious again. "The secretary of the interior," she said slowly. "My, my."

"Our government leaders need to know what's going on out here while Virginia's buying up the land for that park. The Interior Department's in charge of national parks, you know," explained Grandpa.

Carrie drew a deep breath, her curiosity satisfied at last.

"No, I didn't know that," said Mrs. Benton. "Do you think he'll answer you?"

" 'Course he will!" said Grandpa. "In the eyes of the law, one man's as important as another. It doesn't matter whether he lives in Richmond or right here in Mountain View."

"Well, when your answer comes, I'll send Buddy up with it right away," Mrs. Benton said.

Carrie was glad it would be little Buddy, and not his awful brother, Frank, who would be coming to the house with Grandpa's letter.

13

Mrs. Benton looked up when Carrie came into the post office a few days later. "There's a letter for your Grandpa, and it looks mighty important," she said, her small black eyes shining with curiosity. "Nothing from Washington yet, though. Not even a letter from your mama."

Carrie thanked Mrs. Benton and hurried home. Grandpa was on the store porch, talking with some of his customers, but she thrust the letter at him, anyway. "Mrs. Benton thought this looked important," she said. "It's from Richmond."

Well aware of his audience, Grandpa reached into his pocket for his penknife. Slowly he pulled out a blade and slit the envelope. When he unfolded the letter, something fluttered to the ground.

One of the men picked it up. "Looks like a check," he said. Then his eyes widened. "Why, it's for—for almost five thousand dollars!"

"What's that?" spluttered Grandpa, reaching for the check. He looked at it in amazement and then began to read the letter. As he read, his expression changed to anger. "This letter says my land's been condemned and I should make plans to leave here. The check is to—to pay me for this place!" His voice shook.

Carrie's stomach twisted into a knot. Make plans to leave here? Had Grandpa lost his fight?

Somebody whistled and said, "That's a helluva lot more than six dollars an acre!"

Grandpa nodded slowly. "Says here the price was set on the basis of the improvements—I guess that means all the buildings—and the large number of acres in orchards and grass." He looked up angrily. "How in tarnation do they know what I've got here when I sent their appraiser packing?"

"Maybe somebody else told him," suggested one of the men.

Carrie's knees suddenly felt weak, and she sank down on the top step.

"Yeah," said a younger man. "Most everybody knows what all you've got here. All he'd have to do is ask one of your neighbors."

"My neighbors all know how I feel about this," Grandpa snapped. "None of them would have gone behind my back this way!"

Carrie cringed inwardly at his words.

"If they'd told the appraiser anything," Grandpa went

on, "they'd have told him no price anyone can pay will make me leave this mountain."

"Well, looks to me like you're gonna have to leave, 'cause the state's done bought it, Claude," drawled an old man, taking his pipe from his mouth.

"We'll see about that," said Grandpa. "They can't buy it if I don't take their money."

With one quick, deliberate motion, Grandpa ripped the check in half. A gasp went up as the pieces floated to the floor.

"Now, if any of you want to buy something, just get Sarah out of the lunchroom to wait on you. I've got a letter to write," Grandpa said. And nearly tripping over Carrie, he went down the steps and walked quickly to the house.

In the silence that followed, Carrie picked up the torn pieces of the check and slipped them into her pocket. She should have known Grandpa wouldn't let them be forced off their land!

"You got to respect Claude Griffin," one of the younger men said at last. "He don't let anybody push him around."

"It takes some kind of man to go against the plans of the Commonwealth of Virginia and the government of the U.S. of A.," agreed an old farmer. .

Carrie's heart swelled with pride. Grandpa *was* a fighter, just like Grandma said.

Carrie was sitting on the porch swing reading when Grandpa came out of the house. An hour ago, he'd scowled as he took the two halves of the check from her, but he didn't look angry any more.

"Want to walk down to the post office with me, Sunshine?" he asked. "I've got to mail this letter to Richmond."

"I think I'll stay here this time," Carrie said. She didn't want to hear Grandpa tell Mrs. Benton about the traitorous person who had talked to the appraiser behind his back. "What's your letter about?" she asked, her eyes lingering on the envelope in his hand.

"I'm sending them the pieces of the check you brought me and telling them I decline to sell my property," he said. "And I'm suggesting that it would be a good idea to have a place like this in the park. Those tourists are going to get hungry, you know. And their cars are going to need gas."

"Oh, Grandpa! What a wonderful idea!"

"Well, I figure if I can't convince them to let us stay here because it's our right under the Constitution, I'll try to convince them it's to their advantage for us to stay."

Carrie watched Grandpa start down the hill. What a lot of pies they'd need if the park visitors stopped at the lunchroom! Baking with Grandma was fun, but still . . .

14

"Can you ask Aunt Rose not to fight with Grandpa at dinner again today?" Carrie asked after she finished setting the dining room table.

Grandma looked up from stirring the gravy and said, "Whatever are you talking about, Carrie? There's never been any fighting at our table."

"But last time Aunt Rose was here, she said Grandpa ought to get smart and buy a piece of land just outside the park boundary for a new store and gas station, and then he said—"

"Why, that wasn't fighting, Carrie, that was just spirited conversation. Rose and Claude disagree on everything—they always have—and they both love to argue. They have a wonderful time together!"

Carrie looked doubtful. At home nobody argued, and Mama and Daddy didn't raise their voices even when they were angry. She thought of the time Mama had barely spoken to her for a week and she'd never found out why.

When a horn tooted, Carrie went outside to greet her aunt's family. She gave Aunt Rose a halfhearted hug and scowled when she saw the look of understanding that passed between her aunt and uncle as she pulled away. Even the Sunday visits weren't as good as they'd been before the park business complicated everything.

At least it was still fun to be with Amanda, Carrie thought a few minutes later when she and her cousin were swaying gently in the porch swing.

"I'll bet Frank Benton's been too embarrassed about the three-legged race to bother you much lately," Amanda said.

"Don't you remember? He's spending the summer working on his uncle's farm."

"I thought he came home weekends."

"Just that one time." Carrie tried not to think of the Saturday she'd fled to the safety of Annie Burn's house. It still bothered her that she'd let Frank get away with making fun of Grandpa's petition. Somehow, that seemed worse than not being able to stick up for herself.

"What about that other boy, Moses—the cute one that cheered for you in the race?"

Carrie felt herself blushing. "Well, what about him?"

"He is your boyfriend, isn't he?"

"Mama says I'm too young to be interested in boys," Carrie protested.

"My mother says a person is never too young or too old to be interested in the opposite sex," Amanda declared.

Carrie giggled. "Then I guess I've been interested in Moses most all my life," she admitted. "But he just thinks of me as his sisters' friend."

"At least you get to see him when you visit them," Amanda said. "You do, don't you?" she prodded when Carrie didn't respond.

"I'm not visiting Kate and Luanne this summer," Carrie said reluctantly. "It's a long story." She hadn't told her cousin about the trouble between Grandpa and Mr. Edwards because it seemed disloyal to repeat it. She still regretted telling Annie Burns.

Amanda looked hurt. "I thought we didn't keep secrets from each other," she said.

"It's not a secret," Carrie assured her. "It's just something I don't want to talk about."

But it wasn't long before Amanda had teased the story out of her. "I don't blame their father for being angry!" Amanda said when she finished. "Grandpa should go back there and apologize, and when Mama hears about this, I'll bet she'll tell him so!"

Carrie was aghast. "You can't tell your mother, Amanda! We never tell each other's secrets!"

"But you just said it wasn't a secret."

The last thing Carrie wanted was to give Aunt Rose more ammunition to use against Grandpa when they argued about the park. "I'll never tell you anything else as long as I live, if you breathe a word—" She stopped when Grandma opened the screen door.

"When you girls finish your argument, you can get ready for dinner," she said.

"We're not arguing, Grandma. We're having a spirited conversation," Carrie said, hoping she didn't sound too fresh.

"Don't worry, Carrie," Amanda whispered as they went inside. "I won't tell a soul."

The next evening, Carrie watched from the porch until the last of Grandpa's customers started home and he hung out his CLOSED sign. Then she walked over to the store.

Grandpa was standing in front of the cash register, but when Carrie slipped behind the counter to get the broom from the corner, he didn't seem to notice her. In the harsh glare of the light bulb that hung from the ceiling, his face looked tired and worn.

"Are you all right, Grandpa?" Carrie asked tentatively.

The worry lines in his face smoothed out a little when he turned to her. "I didn't hear you come in, Sunshine."

"Are you all right?" she persisted.

Grandpa looked away. "I'm as all right as a man can be when he's standing alone against the kind of odds I'm facing." His jaw was set.

Had Grandpa given up hope, too? Carrie had to know. "Are you worried that you won't be able to save the place, after all?" she asked in a thin voice.

"Of course I'm going to save it!" Grandpa said. "Four generations of Griffins have lived on this land," he went on, "Five, if we count your summers, Carrie. My granddaddy came here with his bride and cut a clearing in the forest for their cabin and a garden. Every year he cleared a little more land for fields and pasture. And then my daddy cut back still more forest and started the orchard and built the house and barn."

His eyes had a faraway look. "I built the store and lunchroom and added to the house. Covered the logs with clapboard shingles and put in the bathroom and a new kitchen for your grandma. Every inch of that house is full of memories for us. And the yard, too," he added. "Your mama and Rose used to play house under that big old boxwood bush by the corner of the front porch."

"So did I," Carrie said, and remembering, she could almost smell the musky scent of boxwood leaves and feel the soft soil beneath its low-hanging boughs. She wished she could crawl under that old boxwood and feel snug and safe, the way she had when she was small.

"A lot of people think I'm crazy to keep on fighting for this place. They think I'm fighting a losing battle."

"I don't think you're crazy, Grandpa," Carrie said. "And I don't think you're going to lose the battle."

Grandpa's face relaxed into a smile. "I don't think I'm going to, either," he said. "This country has been good to the Griffins, and I don't think that's going to change now. 'With liberty and justice for all.' That's what it says in the pledge to our flag. I expect to be treated justly, and I'm going to demand it if I have to appeal all the way to the president. I know my rights, and I won't be deprived of what rightfully belongs to me."

Carrie nodded solemnly and waited a moment to see if Grandpa was finished. When he turned away from her and opened the cash register, she reached for the broom. As she swept the store, Carrie thought about what he'd said. Grandpa knew some people thought he was crazy. But he wasn't going to let that stop him, because he believed in what he was doing. And because he believed in himself. Was that what made him a fighter? she wondered.

15

It was the beginning of August when the CCC boys came back. Glad for something to do, Carrie headed toward the lunchroom. She'd have to wait on them by herself— Grandma was minding the store while Grandpa was on his Thursday morning errands.

As she began serving the men seated at the counter, Carrie was surprised to see how young most of them were. They really *were* almost boys! Some of them smiled at her and she smiled shyly back, but there was no teasing this time. They hadn't forgotten Grandma's warning. While she worked, Carrie listened to their conversations.

"I don't mind getting up before it's light. I don't mind the hard work. I don't even mind the ice-cold showers. But I sure don't like jobs like the one we had to do last night," one young man said.

"What did you have to do?" Carrie asked.

The young man turned to her, and she was surprised to see how very blue his eyes were. "We did an eviction," he said. "Do you know what that is?"

Carrie felt herself blush under his intent gaze. "It's when you move people out because they didn't pay their rent," she answered. She had seen more than one eviction in the city since the Depression began.

The young man nodded. "Except this eviction was up in the park, and the people were tenants who refused to leave after the owner sold the land. The sheriff and his deputies went up there last night and arrested them. Charged them with trespassing on state property. They took us along to move out all their stuff."

"Why did they do it at night?" Carrie asked, carefully sliding a piece of peach pie onto a plate.

"The old farmer and his grown sons kept their guns with 'em and wouldn't let anybody near the place," explained another man. "The sheriff went at night so's to take 'em by surprise."

"The worst thing of all," said a tall dark-haired fellow who had moved up from one of the tables to join the conversation, "is that as soon as everything was out of the house, the sheriff had us set fire to it, and the family saw it burn."

"How horrible!" whispered Carrie, looking up. "I can't believe Sheriff Holmes would make you burn it right in front of them!"

"It was a different sheriff," the newcomer to the counter answered quickly. "This was across the county line, you see."

Somehow, it made Carrie feel a little better to know Sheriff Holmes hadn't been involved in the eviction.

"Any more nights like that and I don't think I'll sign up for another go with the CCC," said a young man at the end of the counter, "even though the money the corps sends home sure is a big help to my mom."

Noticing the puzzled look on Carrie's face, someone explained. "We get paid thirty dollars a month, but they send twenty-five dollars of it home to our families. They just leave us enough to buy a piece of pie now and then."

Everyone was laughing when Grandma came in. She frowned and asked, "Are you having trouble with this crowd?"

Carrie shook her head. "I've served everybody, but the ones at the tables haven't paid yet."

"Well, you know what they had, so you'd better take care of it," Grandma said.

Carrie was glad to be busy. It kept her mind off the terrible story she'd just heard.

At suppertime, Carrie told the story to her grandparents, and Grandpa's eyes didn't leave her face until she was finished. Then he turned to Grandma. "Did you hear anything about this, Sarah?" he demanded.

Grandma nodded. "The boys were talking about it in the store, too. That family had been tenants there a long time. The valley man who owned the land had told the father he could live there for the rest of his life, and one of his sons could have the job after him. That's why they wouldn't leave. They even turned down a chance to have one of those homesteads we heard about. They thought they had permission to stay."

"It's a crime, that's what it is!" Grandpa said, slamming his fist down on the table. "It's a crime that American citizens can be dragged from their homes in the middle of the night by the very officials that are supposed to be protecting them!" He got up and stormed out the back door.

Carrie put her napkin beside her plate and started after him.

"I wouldn't ask him any questions, if I were you," Grandma advised.

Grandpa was in the yard, sawing some boards into four-foot lengths. He called to Carrie as she came out the back door. "Go in the toolshed and bring me my screwdriver and a handful of screws. Long ones."

"These are the longest I could find," Carrie said, holding one up.

"They're fine," Grandpa grunted. "Now bring them along." He picked up the boards and some scraps of lumber and led the way back to the house. Carrie followed him, still wondering what he was doing.

"You stand there and hand me the screws," Grandpa

said, setting down his load just inside the kitchen door.

Carrie and Grandma watched while he made six brackets and screwed them in pairs on either side of the door. He stepped back to admire his work.

"Now we won't have to worry about Sheriff Holmes and his deputies arresting us in our sleep," Grandpa said, slipping a length of board between each pair of brackets to bar the door. "Come along, Carrie, we aren't finished yet," he said, heading for the front hall.

Carrie didn't have to look at Grandma to know that her lips were pressed together in a thin line.

16

The next morning Grandpa brought his rifle to the breakfast table. "From now on, I'll keep this with me during the day," he said, laying it on the floor by his chair.

"Lord, Lord!" cried Grandma, throwing up her hands. "I never thought I'd find myself living in an armed camp!"

"Now, Sarah," said Grandpa sternly, "it's my constitutional right to defend my family and my property, and that's what I'm doing. And when I go to town, I'll leave the gun with you."

"Just a minute, Claude," said Grandma, standing up and putting her hands on her hips. "That's where I draw the line. I'll not be handling any guns. And neither will Carrie," she added quickly as she saw her husband's eyes turn toward their granddaughter.

Carrie breathed a sigh of relief.

"Then I won't be able to go to town," said Grandpa, turning back to his wife. "I'll have to stay here all the time to protect my property."

They began the meal in silence. The clinking of forks against china and the ticking of the big kitchen clock seemed almost unbearable to Carrie, and finally she could stand it no longer. "Is that gun loaded, Grandpa?" she asked.

In answer, he picked up the rifle. Laying it across his lap, he released the clip and held it in his palm. Carrie drew back, and Grandma made a clucking noise with her tongue.

Carrie wished she hadn't asked. The silence was so heavy now that she could hear herself chewing. She was glad when Grandpa took the rifle and left to open the store.

"At this point, staying here seems almost as bad as having to leave," Grandma said flatly.

Carrie didn't want to think about leaving. "Don't worry, Grandma," she said. "Once Grandpa convinces the government to let us keep the place, everything will be the same again."

"No," Grandma said sadly, "even if we did stay, it wouldn't be the same. We'd have the tourist trade, but all the neighbors would be gone." She sighed. "What your grandpa enjoys most about running the store is the socializing. He doesn't realize he'll have lost that even if he wins the right to stay here."

Carrie frowned. "It sounds like you don't want to stay."

"It's been a wonderful place to live," Grandma said wistfully. "Until now."

Their conversation was interrupted by Sport's barking, and Carrie went out to see who had come. A car was parked by the fence, and two men waited outside the gate.

"We've come to talk to Mr. Griffin," one of them called to her. "We're here from Richmond."

"He's at the store," said Carrie, pointing. Grandma joined her on the porch, and they watched the men walk toward the store.

"I'm going over there to see what's happening," Carrie said, hurrying off before her grandmother could respond.

There were no customers on the porch, and to Carrie's surprise, there were no shouts coming from inside the store. She tiptoed up the steps and across the porch to the door. Cupping her hands around her face so she could see through the screen into the darker interior, she saw Grandpa standing behind the counter, listening intently to his visitors.

Carrie heard one of the men say, "So you see, Mr. Griffin, all you have to do is apply for this special permit, and you'll be able to stay here and operate your business." She could scarcely believe her ears! But her rising hope plummeted at Grandpa's next words.

"On a month-to-month basis, you say."

"That's right," said the shorter of the two men. "But you can count on a year or so, at least."

Grandpa shook his head. "I'm not interested in that," he said emphatically. "I'm not asking permission to stay on for a year or so—I'm fighting for my right to stay here for good!"

"But Mr. Griffin," said the taller man, "you have to understand that just isn't possible! The Commonwealth of Virginia has bought your land, and—"

"Now just a minute!" roared Grandpa. "I tore that check in half and sent it back to Richmond! I didn't accept payment, so this place is still mine. And I want you off my property!"

Carrie caught her breath as Grandpa reached under the counter. She'd forgotten about the rifle! Much to her relief, the men looked at each other, shrugged, and started toward the door. Carrie turned and ran back to the house. She joined Grandma, who was sitting on the porch swing, her hands idle in her lap. They watched the two men walk quickly to their car.

"Well, Miss Big Ears, could you hear what went on over there?" Grandma asked as the men drove away.

Carrie had barely finished telling Grandma what she'd heard when a towheaded little boy ran up to the gate waving an envelope. It was Buddy Benton.

"Mr. Griffin got his letter," he called.

"I'll take it to him," said Carrie, jumping to her feet.

"Come on in, Buddy," Grandma called. "I have a little treat for you in the kitchen."

Carrie ran across the lot and burst into the store. "Your letter came, Grandpa," she said breathlessly. "Buddy Benton brought it up."

This time, Grandpa tore the envelope open quickly.

"Is that the letter from Washington you was waitin' for?" asked his only customer, a wiry little man who was counting out the price of a sack of sugar.

"Yep," said Grandpa. "It's from the secretary of the interior. But all he said is that he sent my letter on to the state capital and people from down there would get in touch with me." He snorted. "They were here just before you came in." And he began to describe the visit of the pair from Richmond.

Slowly, Carrie walked back to the house. Already things were different at the store, she thought, remembering what Grandma had said earlier. Just a few weeks ago it was a busy place by this time in the morning. In the kitchen, Buddy was finishing a piece of cake, and when Carrie came in, Grandma cut a slice for her, too.

"Well, thanks for the treat, Mrs. Griffin," Buddy said as he stuffed the last of the cake in his mouth and wiped his hands on his overalls.

"You're welcome, and thank you for bringing up the letter."

At the gate, Buddy looked back and waved. Carrie watched him skip down the road, wondering how it was possible for Frank and Buddy to be from the same family.

At dinnertime, Carrie was unpleasantly aware of Grandpa's rifle lying on the floor by his chair. No one had much to say, and even though the silence didn't feel angry, the way it had that morning, the meal seemed to drag on forever. As soon as she could, Carrie began to clear the table.

From the kitchen window, she saw a car pull in at the gas pumps, and she watched Sheriff Holmes get out, kick his front tire a few times, and then lean against the car.

"Sh—Sheriff Holmes is out there waiting for you, Grandpa," Carrie said in a tight voice.

"I'd better go see what he wants," said Grandpa, finishing his coffee and getting up from the table.

"Do you think he's come to evict us?" asked Carrie, her heart pounding.

"Not all by himself, he hasn't," Grandpa said, leaving his rifle on the floor.

Carrie and Grandma watched from the kitchen window while Grandpa filled the Sheriff's gas tank and pocketed the bill the officer handed him. For several minutes more the men stood beside the car, talking. Carrie remembered how kind the officer had been to Benjamin on the Fourth of July, and she felt a little bit ashamed that she'd been so frightened when he stopped out front.

At last the sheriff drove away and Grandpa came back inside. "Well," he said, "that pair from Richmond drove straight from here to the sheriff's office. Told him to serve papers on me. Eviction papers. They said I was 'uncooperative' and 'refused to comply with state procedures.' "

Grandma and Carrie just stared at him. Carrie's fingernails dug into her palms. The men were right. Grandpa *was* uncooperative, and he *had* refused to do what the state wanted him to.

"I told the sheriff how I'm fighting this thing," Grandpa went on, "and he agreed to give me a couple more weeks."

"Good," said Grandma. "Then you won't have to carry that gun anymore."

"Or barricade the doors at night," Carrie added gratefully. She'd hated the feeling of being locked in.

"Not for a while, anyway. And I'll be able to leave the place and go into town on Thursdays."

"I just thought of something," Grandma said slowly. "You said the sheriff was told to serve eviction papers on you. Does that mean he has to hand you the papers before he can evict us?"

Grandpa thought for a while before he answered. "I believe you have something there, Sarah," he said finally. "We'll remember that."

Carrie went to sit in the porch swing and try to sort things out. Grandpa was pleased that the sheriff was giving him a couple more weeks, but the men from Richmond would have given him a whole year, and he'd sent them away. It just didn't make sense. Then slowly it dawned on her: Grandpa was gambling that something would happen in the next two or three weeks to save their place. If he was right, they'd be able to stay in the mountains permanently. But if he was wrong, they faced eviction. The word made Carrie think of the people who had been moved out at night, the ones who had seen the CCC boys burn their house. Suddenly she felt dizzy.

With her foot, she stopped the motion of the swing, and then she shut her eyes for a moment. When she opened them again, the dizziness had passed. She wasn't going to worry about being evicted, Carrie decided, because in the first place, Grandpa wouldn't let that happen, and in the second place, Sheriff Holmes wouldn't do it to them. Wasn't his visit today proof of that?

17

It was a muggy August afternoon. Carrie sat on the porch, watching an old man slowly climb the steps to the store. When the door slammed shut behind him, she glanced furtively about to make sure no one was in sight.

Casually, she walked toward the far corner of the house, and with another quick glance toward the store and lunchroom, she crawled under the old boxwood bush. She'd been thinking about the quiet haven beneath its limbs ever since Grandpa had reminded her of it almost a week earlier.

The ground was soft, almost dusty, as it had always been. But the cool, dark cavern under the low-hanging branches wasn't as roomy as she remembered. How long had it been since she'd come to this sheltered place? She'd played tea party here with Kate and Luanne one summer, filling her tiny china cups with dirt and piling the small, round leaves on a matching plate for cookies. And one Sunday she and Amanda had hidden here to eat real cookies—cookies they'd stolen from Grandma's kitchen.

Carrie smiled as she thought of her younger self. She broke off some of the spindly dead branches that spiraled the boxwood's trunk and leaned back against it. Hugging her knees, she shut her eyes and let her mind float lazily, just as she had when she was small—when life had been simple. For the first time in weeks, the new park and Grandpa's fight to keep the place were far from her thoughts . . .

Carrie's eyes flew open. Heavy footsteps crossed the porch and came down the steps to the yard, and a gruff voice said, "I haven't seen her all afternoon. When she didn't come over to help me close the store, I just assumed she was with you."

"Where can she be? She's not in her room. I'm worried, Claude. I—"

"Get hold of yourself, Sarah!" Grandpa's voice sounded angry. "She's probably down the road borrowing another magazine from Annie Burns."

"You know she always tells us when she goes anywhere."

Carried held her breath. Peering through the low branches, she could see Grandma's sensible black leather shoes and Grandpa's heavy brown work boots just ten feet away. She hoped they wouldn't find her. How embarrassing it would be if they knew she'd spent the whole afternoon crouched in the dirt, daydreaming like some little kid!

"What are we going to do, Claude?" Grandma's voice sounded quavery.

Carrie watched the heavy boots move closer to the sensible shoes. "Now, Sarah, you go on inside and put the coffeepot on the stove. Sport and I will find her by the time it's perking." Grandpa sounded confident and reassuring.

Carrie saw the sensible shoes turn one way and the boots turn the other. She heard a light step on the porch and the click of the screen door shutting. Then she heard Grandpa call, "C'mon, Sport! Let's find Carrie!"

Hardly a moment later there was a rustling sound followed by a snuffling, and a warm tongue was washing Carrie's face.

"Are you under there, Carrie?" Grandpa sounded incredulous.

Miserable, she crawled out from under the boxwood with Sport playfully nipping at her heels. Grandpa grabbed her arm and jerked her to her feet.

"How dare you worry your grandma like that!" he thundered.

Carrie's eyes filled with tears. She hadn't meant to worry Grandma. Or to make Grandpa angrier than she'd ever seen him, either.

"What were you doing under there?" Grandpa's fingers dug into the soft flesh of Carrie's arm.

Suddenly, she was angry, too. Pulling away, she faced him defiantly. "I was trying to forget!" she shouted. "I was trying to forget about evictions and barricades on the doors and—" She stopped when she saw the stricken look on Grandpa's face. How could she have talked to him like that?

Finally Grandpa spoke. His voice was quiet now. "I've been so worked up about this park business that I never thought about how you must feel. That was wrong of me." He paused and then went on. "Maybe you should stay with your cousins for the rest of the summer. Rose would be glad to have you."

Carrie felt icy cold all over. Grandpa was sending her away! But before she could protest, she heard Grandma's voice. How long had she been there listening?

"No, Claude. Carrie should stay here. What's happening affects her, too, and she'll worry less if she's here with us and knows what's going on." She reached out and brushed a dead twig off Carrie's shoulder.

"But maybe she'd rather—"

"I'd rather be here with you and Grandma! Please don't send me away!" Carrie begged, touching his arm.

Grandpa looked at her searchingly for a moment. Then he took a deep breath and turned to his wife. "Well, Sarah," he said, "didn't I tell you Sport and I would find this girl before your coffee perked?"

After supper, Grandpa excused himself, saying he had an errand to run.

"Where's he going?" Carrie asked as he shut the kitchen door behind him.

"If he'd wanted us to know, he'd have told us, Sunshine."

Carrie saw Grandma try to hide the hint of a smile. "You know where he's going, don't you?"

Grandma nodded.

When Carrie heard the car start, she was even more puzzled. She couldn't imagine what kind of errand he could have at this hour. Everything in town was closed by six. Finally she asked, "When do you think he'll be back?"

"Well after dark, I'd say."

Grandma obviously wasn't going to tell her anything, Carrie thought as she dried the dishes. But it certainly was nothing bad, judging from the cheerful way she was humming while she scrubbed the skillet.

"I think I might bake some oatmeal cookies," Grandma mused as she hung up the dishpan and dried her hands.

"Those are Amanda's favorites," Carrie said. "Can we bake enough to last till the weekend?"

Grandma turned away and opened a cupboard door, but not before Carrie saw that hint of a smile again. She caught her breath. Maybe—no, that would be too good to be true.

"Are we going to make a double batch?" Carrie asked as she set out the measuring cups and bowls.

"One will be enough. There'll be plenty of cookies for Amanda."

Carrie stole a glance at Grandma. Even though she tried not to get her hopes up, she felt little tingles of anticipation. After all, a single batch would never last until Sunday.

"There," Grandma said at last, slipping the cookie sheets into the oven, "these should be ready well before they get here."

Before *they* get here! "Grandpa's gone to get Amanda, hasn't he? Oh, Grandma, do you think Aunt Rose will let her come?"

"Your Grandpa said he'd bring Amanda back with him if he had to kidnap her." Grandma paused and then went on. "What you said this evening, well, that really hit home. He hadn't realized how much this park business was affecting you."

Carrie bit her lip. "I—I don't know what made me say those things. I didn't even know I thought them!"

"It's easy to ignore unpleasant thoughts, and sometimes they don't come out until you're caught off guard, the way you were today. You needed to say what you did, and

Grandpa needed to hear it." Grandma peered into the oven to check on the cookies. Turning back to Carrie she said, "If he'd realized you weren't seeing Kate and Luanne this summer, I think he'd have pressed Rose to let Amanda visit long before this."

"You mean he didn't know that?" Carrie cried.

Grandma shook her head. "Apparently not. He's been pretty wrapped up in his own problems, after all."

"But I've been so lonely without them!" Carrie burst out. "I can't believe he didn't know."

"Did you ever tell him?"

"Of course not! That wouldn't have been nice."

Grandma looked exasperated. "What does 'nice' have to do with it, if it's true? If you deny your own feelings because you don't think they're nice, you're likely to start denying facts you don't think are nice, too."

"I guess you think I'm doing that already," Carrie said slowly.

Putting her arm around Carrie, Grandma said, "Some facts are pretty hard to accept, and it takes some people longer than others to come to grips with them."

"Well, I'm certainly not ready to accept that we're going to have to leave here, if that's what you're hinting at," Carrie said, pulling away. "I won't accept that until Grandpa gives up his fight."

"You don't have to. I think it's a great comfort to your Grandpa to know you believe in him so strongly."

"Does he know you don't believe in him, Grandma?"

"But I do believe in him, Carrie. I believe in *him* even though I don't think what he's doing will make a bit of difference, except maybe to get us moved out sooner than we would have been if he hadn't been labeled a trouble-maker."

Hearing Grandma talk so matter-of-factly about leaving was much worse than anything those state officials said. Cold fear began to steal over Carrie, and she asked, "What will become of us? If they do move us out, that is?" Her voice sounded small and frightened.

"I'm working on that, Carrie," Grandma said, reaching for her potholders. "You don't have to worry."

For once, Carrie found those words reassuring instead of frustrating. She knew Grandma wouldn't keep anything from her that she needed to know.

Grandma pulled the cookie sheets out of the oven, and Carrie helped her transfer the cookies onto wire racks to cool. They'd just finished when Grandpa drove up, honking his horn.

"He's got Amanda with him," Carrie cried, throwing her arms around Grandma in a bear hug. "I just know he has!"

18

"Somebody's heading for the lunchroom, and it's barely nine o'clock," Grandma said the next morning. "You girls better go over so I can finish this ironing while it's still cool."

By the time Carrie and Amanda reached the lunchroom, a lanky young man was sitting at one of the tables, glancing at the handwritten menu. When he looked up, it was all Carrie could do to keep from laughing. The lower part of his face was pink with sunburn, but below his sandy hair his forehead was pale white where it had been protected by his hat.

"May I help you, sir?" Carrie asked, trying hard to keep her face expressionless.

"You can bring me a cup of black coffee and a piece of pie, if the CCC hasn't cleaned you out," the man said, smiling. His voice was rich and pleasing.

How does he know the CCC boys sometimes stop here? Carrie wondered as she went behind the counter to cut the pie. "Did you notice his uniform?" she whispered to Amanda. "He must be some kind of policeman." Then she said aloud, "You can take him a napkin and a fork."

As the girls served their customer, Amanda asked, "Are you some kind of policeman, sir?"

"I'm a ranger in the new Shenandoah National Park," the man said proudly. "I guess that's a little like being a policeman. I have to make sure the people who live in the park don't hunt or trap the wildlife and don't cut down any trees."

"People can live in the park? They don't have to move away?" Carrie asked, looking up hopefully. Had they been worrying for nothing all this time?

"The way I understand it, people who are waiting for the homesteads to be finished can stay after their land's been bought," the ranger said as he bent over his pie. "But everybody else has to leave. Can't very well have people living in a national park, you know."

His cheerful tone, as well as his words, angered Carrie. "I don't see why there has to be a national park, anyway!" she burst out. Her hand flew to her mouth, but she wasn't sorry she'd said it—just surprised.

The ranger raised his pale eyebrows. "We have to preserve the beauty of the Blue Ridge Mountains for future generations of Americans to enjoy," he said seriously.

That sounded like a speech he'd made over and over, Carrie thought resentfully. "But what about *this* generation of Americans—the ones that are being forced out of their homes? What about them?"

"Whoa, there—take it easy!" he said, setting down his coffee cup. "It's like my mother used to say: 'You can't make an omelet without breaking eggs.' "

"What's an omelet got to do with it?" Amanda asked, frowning.

"That's an old saying that means sometimes good things cause a little bit of harm, but it's worth it," the ranger explained.

"Well, it's causing more than a *little* harm, and I don't think the park is worth it," Carrie said coldly. "Now, let me know if you want anything else."

The ranger followed her back to the counter. "If you'd ever been up there on the ridge, I think you'd feel differently," he said earnestly.

"No, I wouldn't," Carrie said with finality. She picked up a dishcloth and began to wipe the counter, pleased that she was finally speaking up.

"I don't think anything would make Carrie feel differently," Amanda said. "You see," she explained, "the government's trying to take this place for the park even though our Grandpa sent back the check."

The ranger blushed under his sunburn. "I didn't know the boundary was this far west—this is my first week on the job, you see," he said apologetically. "Now I understand why you feel the way you do." He frowned as if he were trying to remember something and then asked hesitantly, "Is your grandpa by any chance Claude Griffin?"

The girls nodded.

"Hoo-boy! Let me have another piece of pie and some more coffee while I think this over," he said, resting his elbows on the counter and cupping his chin in his hands.

"That will be forty cents, altogether," Carrie said, setting the pie in front of him while Amanda poured his coffee, splashing some into the saucer. Carrie watched the ranger fold a paper napkin and slip it under the cup. She wished he'd just finish eating and leave.

When he finally pushed away his empty plate the ranger said, "I think if your grandpa could see the waterfalls in White Oak Canyon and the giant hemlock trees in the Limberlost forest, it might help him understand why these mountains should belong to all Americans instead of just a few families."

Carrie looked at him in disbelief. How could he possibly think that?

"Maybe on Sunday I could take you girls and your grandparents to see some of the beauty spots of the park," he persisted.

Beauty spots of the park! Carrie thought scornfully. He sounded like some kind of advertisement.

When the girls didn't answer, the ranger went on. It seemed as though the less they said, the more he felt compelled to fill the silence. "The Skyline Drive—that's what they're calling the road they're building along the crest of the Blue Ridge—isn't paved yet, but I could take you driving on it. The views are absolutely amazing! Why, the CCC boys tell me that on a clear day, you can even see the Washington Monument. I'll bring my binoculars, just in case. What do you think?" he asked, leaning forward hopefully.

Carrie shook her head. She wasn't even tempted, and she could imagine what Grandpa's response to the invitation would be!

The ranger looked disappointed. "Well, you girls talk it over with your grandpa," he said as he counted out his coins. "Next time I stop by, let me know if you've changed your minds."

"Wouldn't you like to see the Washington Monument through his binoculars, Carrie?" Amanda asked as they walked back to the house.

"I've seen the Washington Monument with my bare eyes," Carrie said. "I've even walked up it."

"What about the waterfalls, then? I'll bet you've never seen one of those."

Carrie answered crossly, "I could live all my life without seeing one, if it would stop the government from buying up everybody's land."

"Daddy saw in the paper that all the land for the park has been bought now," Amanda ventured.

"Look, Amanda, do you mind if we talk about something else?" Carrie asked. And then she remembered what Grandma had said the night before about not accepting facts that weren't "nice."

At dinner that noon Amanda asked, "Grandpa, do you think it's possible to see the Washington Monument from up on the ridge?"

"It might be possible with a telescope, but I doubt you could see it with the naked eye."

"Would binoculars work as well as a telescope, do you think?" Amanda persisted. "A ranger told us you might be able to see the monument with binoculars on a clear day."

Grandpa's eyes narrowed. "A ranger, did you say?"

"He's kind of a policeman for the park," Carrie explained, wishing Amanda hadn't brought up the subject.

Grandpa looked from Carrie to Amanda. "And where did you girls meet this park ranger?"

"At the lunchroom. He stopped by this morning because the CCC boys had told him about our pies," Carrie said.

"He wanted to take us all to see some waterfalls up in the park," Amanda added. "He said he could take us along the road they're building up there—they call it the Skyline Drive because it's so high up and the views are so fine."

Grandpa slammed the palm of his hand down on the table so hard the dishes rattled. "How dare that park ranger come here and corrupt my granddaughters on my own property?" he asked Grandma. Then he turned to the girls. "And don't you two know any better than to talk to strangers?"

Carrie and Amanda just stared at him, but Grandma came to their rescue. "Now, Claude, nobody's been corrupted, and I don't really think waiting on a customer at the lunchroom comes under the heading of talking to strangers."

"But we won't wait on him again if you don't want us to," said Amanda. Carrie thought she looked a little frightened.

"You're darn right you won't wait on him again!" Grandpa declared, pushing his chair back from the table. Leaving his meal half eaten, he stormed out of the house.

"Don't worry, girls," Grandma said reassuringly. "You haven't done anything you shouldn't have."

Carrie stared down at her plate. "Amanda should have known better than to say anything about the park."

"Nonsense," said Grandma. "Once you start sticking to 'safe' subjects, next thing you know there'll be nothing left to talk about but the weather."

"Maybe so," Carrie said, "but I don't think she had any business bringing up something that was sure to upset Grandpa."

Amanda looked chastened. "I'll try to remember not to say anything more about the park, Carrie," she said.

Carrie was glad to hear that. She didn't mind when Grandpa was angry about the park business, but when he was angry with her, that was a different story.

19

Amanda looked up from the jigsaw puzzle spread out on the floor of Carrie's room. "What's that noise?" she asked.

"Sounds like somebody hammering out front," Carrie said. "Can you help me find the funny-shaped piece that goes here? It should be mostly green."

But Amanda had pulled back the curtain and was peering outside. "It's Grandpa that's hammering, Carrie. Come and look."

Carrie joined her at the window. "He's putting up a sign," she said, surprised. They watched while he finished nailing it to the outside of the gate and started toward the store with two more signs under his arm. Hurrying to the side window, the girls watched him nail one to the door of the lunchroom and one to the railing around the store porch.

When Grandpa went into the store, the girls ran down the stairs and out the door. Sport came to meet them, tail wagging, and Carrie gave him a hurried pat before she followed Amanda down the walk and out the gate. Wordlessly, they stood staring at the sign. Huge black letters in the center said KEEP OUT! Smaller letters at the top and bottom said VIRGINIA OFFICIALS and SHENANDOAH PARK PEOPLE.

"Well, at least the writing's neat," Amanda said at last.

Carrie was too embarrassed to say anything. She just stared at the awful sign until she heard someone calling.

Then she looked toward the store, where a frail-looking woman was beckoning to them. Two small, grubby children clung to her faded skirt.

"We'd better go see what she wants," Carrie said.

"Can you tell me what that says?" the woman asked, pointing to the sign on the store railing.

"I'll read it for you, ma'am," Amanda said. "The big letters say 'Customers Only,' and the little ones say 'No State or Park Officials.' "

The woman looked puzzled. "Can I go in? I need thread real bad, but I don't go where I ain't welcome."

Carrie said, "You're welcome in the store. Come on, we'll go with you." She started to reach out toward the younger child but changed her mind. His nose was runny, and there was a long, shiny smear on the back of his hand.

Carrie and Amanda held the door open while the woman and her children went inside the store. Then, in silent agreement, they walked over to read the sign on the lunchroom. Large block letters said NO RANGERS ALLOWED INSIDE, and smaller ones added, THIS MEANS YOU!

Carrie was dismayed. At least when Grandpa insulted Kate and Luanne's father it wasn't so public!

"Do you think he put up any others?" Amanda asked.

"We'd better check." Carrie hoped there weren't more signs, but if there were, she had to know what they said.

The girls were careful not to look at the gate when they passed the house. As they started down the road Amanda asked, "How come that woman couldn't read?"

"They don't always have schools way back in the mountains," Carrie said, remembering how Clara Hopkins had to walk all the way to the Mountain View School, and how she couldn't go in bad weather.

"No schools?" Amanda sounded shocked. "You know, Carrie, I think Mama's right that a lot of people in the mountains will be better off when the government moves them out."

Angrily, Carrie turned to her. "What about Grandma and Grandpa? Will they be better off if they have to move? Will they?"

"Of course they won't, Carrie." Amanda sounded hurt. "You know I want them to stay here just as much as you do."

"Well, you don't act much like it," Carrie snapped.

"That's because I know wanting something doesn't make it happen."

Carrie glared at her cousin. "I know that, too, and so does Grandpa. That's why he's fighting for what he wants. For what it's his right to keep."

The girls walked along in silence until Amanda grabbed Carrie's arm and pointed. "Look," she said. "There's another sign."

It was nailed to the dead chestnut tree that marked the southwestern boundary of Grandpa's property. The girls hurried toward it. BEWARE OF FLYING OBJECTS, they read silently. SOME OF THEM MIGHT BE BULLETS.

"Oh, Carrie!" Amanda cried, "do you think he'd really shoot somebody?"

"Of course he wouldn't!" Carrie said.

"Then why—"

Carrie interrupted. "Can't you see? He's really worried

now, and he had to do *something*!" After all, time was getting short—the sheriff had said he'd give them a couple of weeks, and four days of that were gone already.

"Why can't he just accept the inevitable?"

" 'The inevitable'! You must be repeating something you heard your mother say," Carrie said scornfully.

Amanda gave her a long, level look before she said, "I think Mama's right, Carrie."

"And I think you're both terrible, going against Grandpa like this!" Carrie said angrily.

Amanda held her ground. "We aren't going against Grandpa! We just don't agree with what he's doing," she protested.

"That doesn't make any sense!" Carrie burst out.

"Sure it does. I like you, Carrie, but I don't like the way you're acting right now. It's the same kind of thing."

Carrie felt deflated. "I'm sorry, Amanda. I guess I'm upset by these signs and taking it out on you." And as she spoke, Carrie realized that it was true. This park business was affecting her the same way it was affecting Grandpa. How did Grandma manage to stay so calm? she wondered.

A passing car slowed and the driver peered at the sign as he went by. "Do you think that man was scared he'd be shot?" asked Amanda.

Carrie shook her head. "That was our neighbor, Mr. Ward. He knows Grandpa wouldn't shoot anybody." Besides, the look on his face as he read the sign wasn't fear, it was pity.

20

"Who's that boy coming out of the post office?" Amanda asked on Saturday morning.

"That's Kate and Luanne's little brother. We called him Tommy Tattle Tale 'cause he was always spying and telling on us." Carrie thought of the day he'd burst into the lunchroom and found them playing cards. If it hadn't been for him . . .

"Kate and Luanne still aren't allowed to see you?"

Carrie nodded. "And watch—I'll bet Tommy's going to cross the road so he won't have to pass us. Nowadays he always makes a big show of walking on the other side when he goes by our house."

"Then we'll cross over, too, so he'll have to cross back again," Amanda said excitedly.

Carrie shook her head. "Grandma says to ignore him." She carefully avoided looking in Tommy's direction as he passed by on the other side of the road. But before she and Amanda had reached the post office, a stone skimmed past them and bounced into the grass.

"Carrie!" cried Amanda. "That boy is rocking us!"

"Pretend you don't notice," Carrie said, walking faster. But Amanda turned around and shouted, "You cut that out!"

"Beware of flying objects," Tommy yelled, walking backward. "Some of them might be bullets."

Carrie felt a flash of anger. "If your daddy finds out

you're rocking people, you'll be sent away just like Frank Benton was when he got caught rocking cars. Isn't that so, Mr. Edwards?" she hollered, pretending to see Tommy's father coming down the road. When Tommy wheeled around, she yelled out, "Ha, Ha! Made you look!" And then she sang out,

> Made you look, you dirty crook!
> Stole your mother's pocketbook!
> Turned it in, turned it out,
> Turned it into sauerkraut!

Amanda joined in the chant, and they crossed the road and followed Tommy until he stuck his fingers in his ears and started to run. Satisfied, they turned back toward the post office, and Amanda said, "I thought you were going to ignore him."

"Well, if he got away with rocking us, there's no telling what he'd try next," Carrie replied, though she suspected Amanda knew it was Tommy's taunting remark that had made her forget Grandma's advice. Finally, she'd stood up for Grandpa, even though it had been only against Tommy Edwards, and even though she'd had Amanda along for moral support.

Mrs. Benton looked up as the girls came into the post office. Buddy sat on a stool behind the counter with her, drawing on a piece of scrap paper, and he gave Carrie a big smile.

"Well, what was all that commotion about?" the postmistress asked.

"Nothing important," answered Carrie, hoping Mrs. Benton hadn't heard what she'd yelled about Frank. "Any mail for us?"

Mrs. Benton shook her head. "Not today. I hope you two weren't picking on little Tommy Edwards."

Before Carrie could answer, Buddy piped up, "Carrie's nice, Mama. She wouldn't pick on anybody."

As they left the post office, Amanda let the screen door slam behind them. "I don't like that woman," she whispered.

"She's a busybody," Carrie said, starting toward home. "She likes being postmistress so she can find out everybody's business. She always checks to see who Grandpa's writing to and getting letters from, and then she tells the neighbors about 'all the bigwigs Claude writes to.' "

Amanda frowned. "Does that make people think he's putting on airs?"

"Nobody'd ever think that about Grandpa," Carrie said, smiling at the very idea.

"What *do* people think about Grandpa, Carrie?"

Carrie turned to her cousin. "What—what exactly do you mean?" she asked apprehensively.

"Well, do they think he's crazy? Mama says he's acting like a crazy old man, and she doesn't even know about those awful signs."

"How can she say a thing like that about her very own father!" Carrie burst out.

Amanda drew back. "She didn't say he *was* a crazy old man—she only said he was *acting* like one. And you know what, Carrie? I think she's right."

"She's not! She's wrong, wrong, *wrong!*" Carrie cried. "Do crazy people write letters to the editor of the county paper? Do they know the secretary of the interior's the person you write to about national parks? Do crazy people know exactly what their constitutional rights are? Do they? *Do they?*" Her voice shook with anger.

"No," Amanda said, backing away. "No, of course they don't."

They walked the rest of the way home without speaking. Carrie managed not to look at the sign nailed to the dead chestnut at the property line, but this time there was no way she could avoid the one on the gate. Its angry black letters seemed to glare at her. No wonder her cousin thought Grandpa was acting like a crazy old man! Carrie was about to apologize when she saw Moses Edwards coming toward them, carrying a hammer. She waited for him at the gate, but Amanda headed toward the lunchroom.

"If you want me to, I can take down the sign on that old chestnut," Moses said.

"Oh, would you? It's the worst one of all." When Moses nodded but made no move to leave, Carrie said, "I hope you don't think Grandpa's—well, crazy, putting up all these signs." She gestured to the gate.

Moses shook his head. "I'd never think that about Mr. Griffin. This park business has changed him, though, hasn't it?"

"Yes," Carrie said, suddenly aware of how true that was. "Yes, it certainly has."

"Well, I'll go take care of that sign for you now. Some

good did come out of it, though, thanks to you and your cousin," Moses said, grinning.

Carrie thought of Tommy running home with his fingers in his ears, and as she watched Moses walk down the road swinging the hammer, she wished that Buddy Benton was *his* brother and Tommy was *Frank's* brother. Those two deserved each other.

She walked toward the lunchroom, ready to apologize to her cousin, but Amanda called to her cheerfully from behind the counter where she was helping Grandma fill the sugar bowls. "What did Moses want?" she asked.

"He's going to take down the 'Beware of Flying Objects' sign for us," Carrie announced, sitting on one of the stools at the counter. "Do you think we should ask him to take down the others, Grandma? Or maybe just do it ourselves?"

Without looking up, Grandma said, "Your Grandpa needs those signs."

"But don't they embarrass you?"

"No, Carrie, they make me sad."

"Sad?" echoed Amanda.

Grandma hesitated a moment before she asked, "Don't you think it's sad when a man who started out by writing a letter to the editor ends up posting angry signs?"

Slowly, Carrie nodded. That must be what Moses meant about the park business changing Grandpa, she thought. After all, there was no way for him to know how short-tempered and unreasonable Grandpa had become.

Amanda frowned. "Don't travelers ask you about the sign on the lunchroom door?"

"Either that or they make some bright remark. But I just tell them my husband put it there because he's opposed to the new park, and that's usually the end of it." Grandma looked from one girl to the other. "You see, those signs can't embarrass me because I didn't have anything to do with either writing them or putting them up."

"You don't feel it reflects on you?" Carrie asked. Mama was always warning her not to do anything that would reflect badly on her family.

Grandma smiled ruefully. "I used to worry about things like that, but then I decided that since I couldn't control anybody's behavior except my own, I wasn't responsible for anybody's behavior except my own."

That made sense, Carrie thought, wishing Mama felt that way, too. "When did you decide that, Grandma?"

"When all this park business started."

Carrie and Amanda were playing dominoes at one of the tables in the lunchroom later that afternoon when they heard the crunch of footsteps on the gravel outside.

"Remember, Carrie, Grandma said for you to let me wait on the next customer by myself," Amanda said, getting up. "I'm going behind the counter."

When the footsteps stopped outside the door, Carrie peered through the screen and saw the park ranger reading Grandpa's sign, an expression of disbelief on his face. He took off his hat and ran his fingers through his hair, shrugged his shoulders, and put the hat back on. Then he spotted Carrie standing just inside the lunchroom. "I was hoping to buy a piece of that good pie," he said self-consciously, "but since your grandpa doesn't want me here, I'll be going."

He sounded as disappointed as he looked, Carrie thought, noticing that his sunburn had started to peel. "Wait a minute," she said impulsively. "I'll get your pie and you can take it with you." After all, it wasn't his fault he didn't understand how she and Grandpa felt about the park.

"*I'll* get his pie," said Amanda, who had joined Carrie at the door. She headed for the counter again, and Carrie slipped outside to join the ranger.

"I'm sorry about the sign," she said lamely.

The ranger nodded. "I'm sorry, too. I'm going to miss your pies."

There was an awkward silence, and Carrie was glad when her cousin brought out an enormous slice of peach pie.

"Here," Amanda said, handing it to the ranger. "And don't worry about the plate. It's a cracked one Grandma was going to throw away."

The ranger's eyes lit up as he reached for it. "This is wonderful!" he said. "I've been thinking about your pies ever since I was here before. How much do I owe you?"

"Nothing," Carrie said quickly.

And Amanda added, "It's a present—to make up for that mean sign."

Before the ranger could answer, a voice bellowed, "Can't you read?" The ranger took a step backward as Grandpa confronted him. "How dare you come here and corrupt my granddaughters? The secretary of the interior's going to hear about this! Now get out of here, and don't come back again!"

His face red and contorted with rage, Grandpa shook his fist at the ranger, and the young man, who must have been almost a foot taller, leaned backward, trying to balance his plate of pie. He looked so comical Carrie would have laughed if she hadn't been so embarrassed.

The ranger swallowed hard. Then, glancing apologetically at the girls, he turned and walked to his car. Carrie was glad Grandpa hadn't made him leave his pie.

"And now, young ladies," Grandpa began, glaring at Carrie and Amanda, "just what do you think—" He broke off and looked toward the house.

The girls looked, too. Grandma was standing in the yard, waving. "Can you come here, Claude? I need you right away!" Without another word to the girls, Grandpa started toward the house.

"I'm glad Grandma called when she did," Amanda said. "What do you think she needs him for?"

"To tell him to leave us alone, most likely," Carrie said. "I'm glad the ranger got his pie, aren't you?"

Amanda nodded. "Do you think he's going to come back?" she asked.

"Who, the ranger?"

"No, Grandpa."

Why, she really is afraid of him, Carrie thought. "You don't have to worry," she said reassuringly. "He's not going to come back, and he won't say anything to us later, either."

Amanda gave a sigh of relief. "Then let's go inside and finish our dominoes game. You know, Carrie," she confided, opening the door, "I'm almost glad tomorrow's Sunday and I'll be going home with the folks after dinner. "I've had a good time with you and Grandma this week, but . . ." Her voice drifted away.

Slowly, Carrie followed her cousin inside, wondering if Grandpa's fight was really worth it. Things had been getting worse and worse, ever since the sheriff's visit. But then she thought of what her grandmother had said earlier. Grandpa *had* to fight. Squaring her shoulders, Carrie decided she would stand by him, no matter what.

21

The house seemed quiet and empty with Amanda gone, and Carrie was feeling a little sorry for herself. Grandma was minding the store that afternoon while Grandpa wrote another letter, so Carrie had only her own thoughts for company while she washed the dishes. Grandpa was still writing when Carrie finished drying the last of the pots and pans, and he didn't seem to notice when she sat down opposite him with her pencil and tablet. She hadn't written home during the week Amanda visited, and she knew Mama would be waiting to hear from her.

But what could she say? *Dear Mama, I am fine, and so are Grandma and Grandpa. Sorry I didn't write last week, but Amanda was here. We had a lot of fun.* She thought back over her cousin's visit for something she could tell Mama about, but it was all too mixed in with the park business. It seemed like everything that happened this summer was somehow connected with the park.

Carrie glanced across the table and was surprised to see that Grandpa was writing in pencil, too, erasing a word here and there and sometimes changing a whole line. This letter must be really important, Carrie thought as she watched. At last he seemed satisfied with what he'd written. He read it over and then reached for his ink bottle and pen.

Resolutely, Carrie bent over her paper. *I guess Grandma wrote you about the park business. Grandpa is worried about losing the place, and he's writing a letter to somebody about it now.* Looking up, she thought a minute more and then wrote, *I worry about it too, but there isn't anything I can do.* So there! she thought, and then quickly, before she could change her mind and erase what she'd written, she added, *Tell Daddy I said Hi. Love, Carrie*, and sealed it into an envelope. She finished addressing it at the same time Grandpa finished copying his letter.

She watched while he addressed his envelope, trying in vain to read it upside down. "Want me to mail that for you when I mail my letter to Mama?" she asked.

"I'd appreciate that," he said, smiling. "Here's the stamp money." He counted out the pennies, laid them on the envelope, and pushed it all across the table toward her.

Carrie gasped when she saw the address. The President of the United States! No wonder he'd made a draft of his letter! "Can just anybody write to the president?" she asked in amazement.

"He's the president of all the people, Carrie."

"Do you think he'll help us?"

"I don't know, but I'm willing to try anything that

might improve our chances of keeping this place. Nothing I've done so far has brought results, so now I'm going right to the top."

Carrie didn't know what to say to that, so she simply took the two envelopes and the stamp money and started off for the post office. The blacktop road was hot under her feet, but she barely noticed. She was too busy wondering whether the president would help them. She was glad Grandpa had written to him—it made a lot more sense than putting up those signs.

"What? Two letters for Washington today?" Mrs. Benton asked, looking up from her knitting when Carrie came in.

"Yes, ma'am," Carrie answered politely, putting her pennies on the high counter.

"One for your mama and one for the president, I suppose," Mrs. Benton joked, handing her the stamps.

"Yes, ma'am," Carrie answered as she licked the stamps and carefully stuck them on the envelopes.

Mrs. Benton's chuckle ended in a choking sound when she saw the address on Grandpa's envelope, and Carrie hurried out the door, trying not to laugh aloud.

Feeling more lighthearted than she had for weeks, she walked up the road and went straight to the lunchroom. She sat down at the counter and said, "I'll have a glass of iced tea, please, Mrs. Griffin."

"Oh, I'm so sorry, miss. We're fresh out," Grandma said. Then, smiling at Carrie's crestfallen expression, she went to the icebox for the pitcher.

Carrie sipped the cold drink and told Grandma about

Grandpa's letter, repeating her conversation with Mrs. Benton. "Do you think writing to the president will help?" she asked.

"Well, it can't hurt, can it?" Grandma replied. Then she said, "Let's go over to the store and choose material for a couple of dresses for you. I've let out all your hems, but you're growing so fast everything's too short again. And getting a wee bit tight across the chest, too."

Carrie crossed her fingers, hoping she wouldn't be the smallest—and flattest—girl in her class again this year. Waving to Grandpa, who was pumping gas into a farm truck, she followed Grandma over to the store. As she started up the steps, she paused and frowned. "Do you smell smoke?" she asked.

"I've smelled it off and on all afternoon. Probably just somebody burning trash," Grandma answered, holding the door for Carrie and then leading the way to the back of the store, where bolts of cloth were on display. "This blue plaid would be nice for school, don't you think?" she suggested.

Carrie nodded, but she wasn't ready to think about school yet. She looked up when the door banged shut behind Grandpa.

"CCC truck just pulled in," he said.

"Then we'd better go on over to the lunchroom," Grandma said, putting the cloth away. Carrie followed her out the door. The CCC boys were clustered around Grandpa's sign, and they looked inquiringly at Grandma.

"Go right on in," she said. "That sign isn't meant for you."

"I didn't think so," one of them said. "We work too

hard and earn too little for anybody to mistake us for officials." He and a few of the others went up the steps and into the store while the rest followed Grandma and Carrie to the lunchroom. Carrie saw one of the men nudge another and point to the sign on the door, but no one said anything about it.

The blue-eyed young man who had told the story of the eviction smiled at Carrie as he sat down at the counter. "Well, we haven't had any more of that night work since we were here last," he said, answering her unasked question.

"But the daytime work is sure keeping us busy," chimed in his dark-haired friend. "We just helped your neighbors up the road move to their new place," he added.

"You mean the Edwards family?" Carrie asked in dismay.

The man shook his head. "It was the Wards. Took us since early this morning to move all their stuff."

"Lizzy Ward stopped by yesterday and told me they'd be going soon," Grandma said, shaking her head sadly as she poured the coffee. "We've been neighbors for almost thirty-five years."

Kate and Luanne had been her friends for almost their whole lives, Carrie thought. It would be terrible if she couldn't tell them good-bye! She felt a wave of anger at Mr. Edwards—and at Grandpa.

"Well, we've got a lot of other jobs scheduled that will bring us past here, so your assistant pie baker is going to be busy," the dark-haired man said, winking at Carrie. Then he turned to his friend. "Come on, Tom, let's go back over to the store."

Carrie watched them leave. So the blue-eyed young man's name was Tom.

She was wiping off the tables when the door to the lunchroom opened and Moses Edwards came in. "Kate and Luanne sent you this," he said, handing her a folded piece of lined paper.

Carrie took it from him eagerly, but her heart fell when she saw how short it was.

Dear Carrie,

We can't come to say goodby, so we asked Moses to give you this letter. We're moveing tomorrow. Its to bad we'll never see each other again.

Your friends,
Kate and Luanne

The words blurred before Carrie's eyes. Seeing it in writing made it seem so much more real than just knowing it was going to happen. "Thanks for bringing this," she said without looking up, relieved that her voice was steady.

"If you want, I can stay while you write an answer," Moses said.

"Sit down, and I'll get you a bottle of pop to drink while you wait," Carrie said, blinking rapidly.

From behind the counter Grandma said, "Maybe Moses would like this last piece of pie, too."

Carrie couldn't help but notice how his eyes shone when she brought it to him. Mama must be right that the best way to a man's heart is through his stomach, she thought as she hurried to the house to find a pencil and the tablet she used for her letters home.

Back in the lunchroom a few minutes later, she sat down across the table from Moses. Very much aware of his presence, she began to write:

Dear Kate and Luanne,
      I'm glad you sent the note with Moses.
      I'll miss you when you're gone. I wish this summer had been like all our other summers.

Frowning, she read over what she'd written and tried to think of something to add, beginning to understand why Kate and Luanne's note hadn't been any longer. Then, fearing that Moses was tired of waiting, she quickly signed her name, tore the sheet from her tablet, and handed it to him.

He folded it in half without looking at it and slipped it into his shirt pocket. "When are you leaving, Carrie?" he asked as he stood up.

"I always stay till right before school starts," she answered, surprised that he didn't remember from other years.

"I mean, when are you and your grandparents leaving the mountain?"

Carrie felt like she had the time the dodge ball hit her in the stomach and knocked the wind out of her. She just stared at him, not knowing what to say.

"I—I'm sorry, Carrie," he mumbled, looking down at the floor. "I didn't know you were still counting on staying here." He hesitated a moment, and then he met her eyes. "I don't want to leave, either," he said. "But this time tomorrow, our place will be ashes, just like the Wards' place is now." Without another word, he turned and left.

So that was why she'd smelled smoke this afternoon, Carrie thought as the screen door slammed behind Moses. She slumped down in her chair, staring at her friends' note without really seeing it. When Grandma came from behind the counter and sat down across from her, Carrie looked up. "I don't think I could stand it if we had to move away from here, Grandma," she whispered.

"It would be hard for you," Grandma said, "but you could stand it. You'll never know how strong you are, Carrie, till you have to face up to something you thought you couldn't stand."

Carrie looked at her grandmother and realized that was what she'd been doing all along—facing up! Suddenly, she was confused. She'd thought Grandpa was the strong one, sticking up for his rights and fighting to keep this place. Could she have been wrong?

22

After supper, Grandma suggested that they take a walk up the road and enjoy the cool August evening. Carrie wanted to stay home, but Grandma insisted that she come. So she dragged along behind her grandparents, wishing she could forget her conversation with Moses that afternoon and trying not to think of the haunted look in his eyes when he'd said, "I don't want to go, either."

As they neared the Wards' place, the stench of smoke hung heavy in the air. "I guess your CCC boys burned the buildings after they'd moved everything out," Grandpa said bitterly.

A morbid curiosity made Carrie walk a little faster, but she was unprepared for what she saw when they rounded the curve. She gasped at the sight of the charred ruin. All that remained of the stately house were the chimneys at either end and the stone foundation between them.

Grandma broke the silence. "That was such a fine place," she said. "What a pity it had to be destroyed."

"Jim Ward might have saved it if he'd had the gumption to try," Grandpa said gruffly.

Grandma stooped to pick up a curved fragment of blue china. "This looks like a piece of that bowl Lizzy's mother left her. The CCC boys must have dropped it." She shook her head sadly.

The grass around the house and the sheds and other buildings was seared black by the flames, leaving a strange pattern of light and dark rectangles on the ground, and a row of charred fence posts outlined the yard. A chill of foreboding gripped Carrie, and she saw in her mind's eye the blackened trunks of the poplars in her grandparents' yard. Was that what lay ahead? Could the president's help possibly come in time to save them?

All at once, Carrie knew what she had to do. "I don't want to go any further," she said. "I'm going back by myself."

"We'll all go back, Carrie," Grandpa said, resting a comforting hand on her shoulder.

Carrie looked pleadingly at her grandmother.

"I'd like to walk on a bit farther, Claude," Grandma said.

Carrie started down the road before Grandpa could reply. As soon as she rounded the curve, she began to run, hardly noticing the sharp little rocks under her bare feet. She was gasping for breath and had a stitch in her side long before the back of the store building and the kitchen end of the house came into view, but she kept on running. She would need every possible minute to carry out her plan.

Back at the house, Carrie snatched the key from its nail in the kitchen and then ran over to the store. She felt the latch snap back as the key turned in the lock, and she pushed the heavy door open. Standing on a box she dragged from behind the counter, she reached up to pull the string that dangled from the ceiling light.

The public phone hung on the wall to the right of the door. Carrie's mouth was dry and her heart pounded as she lifted the receiver and turned the crank on the side of the phone. She held her breath while she waited for the operator to answer.

At last a voice crackled loudly in her ear: "Central."

Carrie took a deep breath and said, "Operator, I need to call Washington, D.C."

"Where are you calling from, dear?"

"From Griffin's Store."

"Griffin's Store? Isn't the store closed?"

"Yes, ma'am." Carrie's hands were damp, and drops of perspiration trickled down between her shoulder blades. "The store *is* closed, but I'm Mr. Griffin's granddaughter."

"Oh, you must be Carrie. This is Mrs. Stokes. I met you in town with your Grandpa last summer. Give me your mama's number, and I'll put your call through as quickly as I can."

"I'm not calling my mother, Mrs. Stokes," Carrie said, adding in a rush, "I'm calling President Roosevelt."

There was silence at the other end of the line for several seconds before the operator said, "The President of the United States doesn't have time to talk to children."

Carrie's fingers clenched tighter around the receiver. "He's president of all the people, and I have to talk to him about something important," she said in a steady voice. Somehow, it was easier to stand up to somebody she couldn't see.

"Now, Carrie, I think I know what it is that's so important, but even your grandpa wouldn't try to call the president to talk about it. I want you to hang up now, and we'll forget all about this. It'll be our little secret, and I—"

Carrie couldn't bear to listen to the patronizing voice any longer. She slammed the receiver onto its cradle. "Shut up!" she shouted. "Shut up! Shut up! Shut up!"

Her words echoed in the silence of the empty store, and she clapped her hands over her mouth. What would Grandpa think if he'd heard her? And what would he say if—no, *when*—he found out she'd hung up on the operator? She sank to the floor and began to sob.

That was how Grandpa found her. "What's the matter, Carrie?" he asked, squatting down beside her. Little by little, he coaxed the story out of her.

"She treated me like I was Buddy Benton's age!" Carrie

said indignantly. "It'll be our little secret," she mimicked.

Grandpa snorted. "Not much chance of that! The only thing that spreads the news faster than the Bell Telephone System is the Frances Stokes tell-a-woman system!" He laughed heartily at his own joke, but Carrie started to cry again at the thought of everyone for miles around hearing how Claude Griffin's rude granddaughter had hung up on the operator. Her only comfort was that she'd hung up before she shouted her angry words.

"Did she actually say 'Even your grandpa wouldn't try to call the president'?"

Carried nodded through her tears.

"Well, we'll see about that!" Grandpa reached for the phone. He turned the crank, waited a few seconds and turned it again, motioning for Carrie to stand close beside him. She heard the operator answer, and then Grandpa spoke into the mouthpiece.

"Frances, this is Claude Griffin."

"Oh, hello, Claude. Your phone's been keeping me busy this evening!"

So much for "our little secret," Carrie thought as Grandpa said, "So I understand. I need to place a call to Washington, D.C., Frances. To the White House."

There was a long pause, and then Carrie heard the operator say with great formality, "I'll ring you back when you call has been completed, Mr. Griffin."

Grandpa replaced the receiver and walked over to lean against the counter, idly whistling between his teeth.

"What are you going to say to the president?" Carrie asked.

"What were *you* going to say to him, Sunshine?"

Before she could reply, the phone rang its two shrill rings. Grandpa cleared his throat and answered it, and Carrie leaned close so she could hear.

"I'm sorry, Mr. Griffin," the operator said coldly, "but the White House office is closed."

"Well, I'm much obliged to you for putting through the call, Frances," Grandpa said. "My granddaughter said she had some trouble when she tried earlier."

He hung up without waiting for a response and looked at Carrie with satisfaction.

"I never thought about the president's office being closed," Carrie said, rubbing a bruise on her heel and feeling less guilty about hanging up. "I guess it didn't matter, after all, that Mrs. Stokes wouldn't put through my call."

Grandpa shook his head. "It's the principle of the thing that's important. That woman's job is to help people make calls, not to censor them."

Carrie followed Grandpa back to the house. She was glad she'd tried to call the president, even if nothing had come of it. It had felt good to be *doing* something instead of waiting helplessly to see what would happen next.

23

On the way home from the post office a few days later, Carrie saw someone coming toward her, and squinting into the sun, she recognized Frank Benton. What was he doing home from his uncle's farm? She glanced wistfully at the Burns's gate but forced herself to walk past it. She wasn't going to hide behind Annie's skirts again. This time, she'd catch Frank off guard by speaking to him first.

But what should she say? Maybe she should call out, "Why, Frankie, I haven't seen you since the Fourth of July!" She grinned in spite of her nervousness. Mrs. Benton had told Grandma how everyone had teased Frank and his red-haired cousin for losing to the only girls in the three-legged race.

As the distance between them narrowed, Carrie forgot her brave resolve to speak first. She swallowed hard when Frank stopped in front of her, his hands on his hips and one cheek bulging. "Well," he said, "if it ain't little Miss Carrie from Washington Dee Cee. What's that you have there, Miss Carrie? A letter from the president?"

"Oh, hello, Frank," she said, ignoring his mocking tone. "No, it's just a letter from my mother." She was pleased that her voice sounded normal.

"I see," Frank said, taking a red jawbreaker from his mouth, inspecting it carefully, and then popping it back in. "I guess you and the president talk on the phone nowadays instead of writing."

Carrie fought down the old familiar feelings of helplessness and made herself answer calmly. "Actually, we've never talked *or* corresponded."

Taking the candy out of his mouth again, Frank held it affectedly between his thumb and forefinger. "What?" he said. "Never even cor-re-spond-ed?"

"That's right," Carrie replied, looking him straight in the eye, "never even corresponded." She was doing it! She was standing up to Frank Benton!

Frank looked away first. Gazing skyward he said, "I guess it's just your crazy old grandfather that cor-re-sponds with the president and all those other important people in Washington Dee Cee. And in Richmond, too," he added.

For a moment Carrie could hardly see. A red haze of anger engulfed her, blocking her vision and nearly smothering her. Before she realized what she was doing, she rushed at Frank and gave him a mighty shove. "Don't you dare talk like that about my grandfather!" she cried. "Don't you dare!"

He staggered backward, trying to keep his balance. "Hey! What do you think you're doing?"

Carrie stood glaring at him, her face flushed, clenching and unclenching her fists. "Did you hear what I said to you, Frank Benton?" she hissed. "Did you hear what I said?"

"Aw, look what you done," Frank said, ignoring her question and leaning down to pick up something off the roadside. "You've gone and spoiled my jawbreaker!"

Carrie looked from Frank to the dust-covered sphere he held. "That's too bad, Frank," she said in her most sympathetic voice. "But I'm sure my 'crazy old grandfather' will give you another one if you go back to the store and tell him what happened."

Frank blushed beet red. Carrie watched the color spread clear to the roots of his wheat-colored hair. Suddenly turning away from her, he drew back his arm and hurled the jawbreaker across the highway. Then he jammed his hands in his overalls pockets and started home, cursing as he went.

Carrie stared after him until he was out of sight, knowing he'd feel her eyes burning into his back. Then, her anger giving way to a mixture of triumph and satisfaction, she picked up her letter from where it had fallen and started home again.

In the kitchen, she poured herself a glass of iced tea and settled down at the table to read Mama's letter.

Dear Carrie,

I'm sorry you're not having your usual carefree summer with Grandma and Grandpa. At first I wondered if maybe you should come home, but then life isn't easy here in the city, either, with this Depression. And at least you're getting fresh vegetables and lots of milk to drink.

There was more, but Carrie stopped and read the first paragraph again. This wasn't like any other letter she'd ever gotten from home! It was so—well, so *honest*. But then, Carrie remembered, her last letter to Mama had been honest, too, when she'd admitted she was worried about the park business.

Carrie looked up when the kitchen door opened and

Grandma came in from hanging out the wash. "I saw Frank Benton leave the store a little while ago," she said. "If you met up with him, I hope he didn't give you any trouble. That boy has a nasty mouth on him."

Carrie grinned in spite of herself. "You don't have to worry. I'm not afraid of that scrawny, knobby-elbowed kid anymore," she said. Immediately, she wished she'd left off the *anymore*.

Grandma looked at her closely for a minute, then nodded knowingly. "Good for you, Carrie," she said. "Good for you."

24

Carrie and Grandma were rolling out pie dough a few days later when Carrie glanced out the kitchen window and saw the sheriff's car pull up in front of the store. "Look, there's Sheriff Holmes again," she said. Grandma joined her at the window, and they watched him get out of his car and start up the steps with a piece of paper. Grandpa, who had been standing on the porch talking to an old man, suddenly ran inside the store, slamming the heavy wooden door behind him.

The sheriff pounded on the door and shouted something.

"That paper he's got!" Carrie cried. "It must be the eviction notice!" She ran to shut the front door, barricading it with the boards Grandpa had left standing nearby, and Grandma hurried to bar the kitchen door.

By the time they got back to the window, the sheriff was walking toward the house. "Do you think he'll try to break down the door?" Carrie asked anxiously.

"Do you think Sport will let him past the gate?"

Why, Grandpa hadn't needed that awful KEEP OUT sign at all, Carrie realized. At least, not to keep anybody out.

Sport began to bark, and they heard the sheriff calling, "Mrs. Griffin? Mrs. Griffin, can you come out here for a minute?"

It seemed like a long time before Sport quieted down and they knew Sheriff Holmes had given up. From the kitchen window they watched him walk back to the store and heard him shouting through the door again. After the sheriff drove off, Grandpa came out and joined the customer he'd been talking to earlier.

"What do you think they're saying?" asked Carrie.

"You stay right here, now," Grandma said sharply. "We'll hear about it soon enough."

Silently, Grandma and Carrie finished the pies and put them in the oven. They were cleaning up the kitchen when they heard someone banging on the door. Carrie was terrified until Grandma said, "Go let your Grandpa in."

"If a bear had been chasing me, he'd have got me for sure," Grandpa said after Carrie had removed the boards and unlocked the door. His hearty tone of voice sounded false to Carrie, and she frowned as she followed him back to the kitchen.

"Well, Sarah," he said with a deep sigh, "I guess my time has run out, far as the sheriff is concerned."

"Didn't you tell him the president hasn't answered your letter yet and you need more time?" cried Carrie.

Grandpa shook his head. "It's out of the sheriff's hands now. He told me the state has threatened to hold him in contempt of court if he doesn't serve that paper on us."

Carrie didn't know what "contempt of court" meant, but she could tell from the look on Grandpa's face that it must be serious.

"So he'll be back," said Grandma.

Grandpa nodded grimly. "He'll be back. I'll keep an eye out for his car and lock myself in the store if I see him coming. But I'm closing the lunchroom. I don't want the sheriff to have a chance to serve those papers on you while we're still waiting to hear from the president."

"Let's call his office again, right now!" Carrie urged. She hated to think of Grandpa hiding from the sheriff.

"I tried calling just before I came over here, but I couldn't get through," Grandpa said. "Looks like we'll have to wait for the letter. I want it in writing, anyway. And while we're waiting, you'll have to do your grandma's outdoor work, because I want her to stay in the house."

"Now, Claude, you know Sport won't let anybody he doesn't know past the gate. Didn't you hear him today? We wouldn't have needed your barricades."

Grandpa scowled. "From now on, I want Sport tied. I hate to think what might happen if one of those deputies tried to come in the yard and Sport attacked him. And now, Sarah," Grandpa said, pushing his chair back from the table, "if there's anything you need at the lunchroom, better go get it. And Carrie, you can move Sport's water dish over by the toolshed while I find a rope."

Carrie stayed a few minutes to comfort Sport after Grandpa tied him to a tree by the toolshed. She wished Grandpa would keep on calling the president. Couldn't he see there might not be time to get his answer in writing? When Carrie saw Grandma coming back from giving the lunchroom a final check, she went to meet her.

"I never thought I'd see the day when I was a prisoner in my own home," Grandma grumbled.

Carrie didn't know what to say to that, so she asked, "With the lunchroom closed, what are we going to do with all the pies?"

And then they both cried out, "The pies!" and ran toward the house. They could smell the burning pastry before they got there, and when Grandma opened the oven door the smoke poured out. After it cleared a little, they could see where the fruit had bubbled over and burnt onto the bottom of the oven.

"Well," said Grandma, surveying the charred mess, "at least now we know what to do with all those pies. We're going to throw them out."

Carrie giggled in spite of herself.

"And when this mess is cleaned up," Grandma went on, "I'll start to work on your new dresses."

25

After breakfast the next morning, Carrie fed Grandma's chickens, talking to them quietly as they clucked and scratched around her feet, pecking at the cracked grain. Then she went to comfort Sport. He lay on the dirt, his head between his paws, and when Carrie came toward him he thumped his tail once.

"You poor thing," she said, sitting down beside him. "You haven't done anything wrong—you're a good dog." Recognizing the words "good dog," he put his head in her lap and wagged his tail more enthusiastically.

Carrie was still petting him when a battered old Ford drove up to the gas pumps. Idly, she watched Grandpa come out of the store and walk toward the car. But just before he reached it, the doors flew open and three men sprang out. Carrie gasped when she saw them grab Grandpa's arms and push him up against one of the gas pumps. Jumping to her feet, she ran to the house and burst through the kitchen door, crying, "Grandma! Grandma!"

Grandma hurried down from upstairs, where she'd been sewing. "What is it? What's wrong?"

"Some men have got Grandpa!" Her heart pounding wildly, Carrie tore at the boards that barred the front door. She and Grandma ran onto the porch just in time to see the men push Grandpa—handcuffed!—into the car and climb in with him.

The driver backed up until he was opposite the gate. "I'm sorry about this, Mrs. Griffin. I really am," he called.

Grandma pressed her lips together and didn't answer, and after a moment he drove away.

"That was Sheriff Holmes!" Carrie cried.

"And the others were his deputies," Grandma said. "They came in their regular clothes, and in an ordinary car, so they could trick your grandpa!" Her voice shook with anger.

Carrie felt betrayed. Sheriff Holmes and his men had tricked Grandpa! Where were they taking him? What did it all mean? Could they put somebody in jail for being uncooperative? Carrie's thoughts were a confused jumble. She and Grandma were still standing at the bottom of the porch steps, staring bleakly down the road, when the brown CCC truck pulled in. But this time, instead of stopping in front of the store, the driver parked by the gate. The CCC boys climbed out of the back and stood around awkwardly, looking at the ground.

"I'm sorry, boys," Grandma said, walking over to them. "We're closed today. Both the store and the lunchroom."

The young men continued to study the ground, and one of them kicked at a large piece of gravel. Finally the truck driver, an older man, spoke. "We know, ma'am," he said. "We've come to help you move. I have our orders right here."

"But we haven't heard from President Roosevelt yet!" Carrie cried. Several of the CCC boys glanced at her curiously, and she felt her face flush with embarrassment.

The truck driver held out his official-looking paper, and when Grandma reached for it, Carrie grabbed her arm.

"No!" she cried. "We can go inside and bar the doors." She was sure none of the CCC boys would try to stop them.

"No, Carrie," Grandma said firmly, "there's no use postponing the inevitable." She squared her shoulders. "I've been expecting this," she added.

Carrie felt cold all over, even though the late August sun was beating down on her. How could this be happening? The CCC man cleared his throat. "We're supposed to have everything out of the house—and the store and lunchroom—by noon," he said. "I guess we'll have to stack it all in the lot here."

Carrie saw Tom step forward. "We're real sorry about this, ma'am," he said.

Grandma's face was pale, but her voice was steady. "You're just doing your job," she said.

"Some of us are going to stay here and guard your things till you decide where we should take them," Tom went on.

"That's mighty kind of you," Grandma said quietly.

Carrie wished she could thank Tom, too, but her throat felt strained and tight. She didn't want to cry in front of the CCC boys. She wouldn't!

"All right, boys. You know what to do," said the driver, and they moved slowly toward the house.

"We brought boxes for your dishes and other kitchen things, Mrs. Griffin," said the driver. "Do you want to pack them, or shall we do it for you?"

Carrie held her breath, thinking of the fragment of blue china they'd found in the flame-seared grass at the Wards' place.

"I'll do it," Grandma said. "Come on, Carrie. I'll need your help."

Woodenly, Carrie followed her to the house. At the door, they had to stand aside while two CCC boys carried out the spare room bureau. Behind them came another pair, carrying a mattress with the bedding still on it. And in the kitchen, two young men were lifting up the table.

"We're going to need to set these boxes on that while we pack the china," Grandma said. Her voice sounded polite but very far away.

"We'll get it later, then," mumbled one of the men.

"We're real sorry about all this, ma'am," said the other, backing out of the kitchen.

Grandma acknowledged their words with a quick nod, and she and Carrie set silently to work. As Carrie packed the mixing bowls and measuring cups in one of the boxes, she realized that she and Grandma would never again work side by side, baking pies for the lunchroom. Her throat tightened, and she stole a glance at Grandma, who was carefully wrapping her favorite platter in a dish towel.

Grandma looked up, and when their eyes met she said, "Don't think about it, Carrie. Just do what has to be done, and don't think about it."

Obediently, Carrie tried to keep her mind blank, concentrating on the repetitive movements of her hands. All the china and most of the pots and pans were packed by the time she heard a car stop outside. "Maybe they've brought Grandpa back," she said, looking up.

Grandma reached across the table and took both of Carrie's hands in hers. "Remember, Carrie," she said, "your grandpa did everything possible to save this place. There's nothing more he can do. Nothing."

Carrie pulled away and ran to the front door. She got there in time to see Grandpa climb out of the sheriff's car, but something about the way he moved stopped her from going out to meet him. She watched from inside the screen door while he stood looking at the furniture that lined the side of the highway. Then his shoulders slumped, and he sank down onto one of the parlor chairs.

Carrie swallowed hard. Grandma was right. There was nothing more that he could do, and he knew it. Carrie turned and walked slowly to the kitchen. "Grandpa's back, but he's just sitting there like—like—" she searched for words—"like a stranger," she finished lamely. "What are we going to do?"

"We're going to go out there and sit with him," Grandma said, closing the last box.

Carrie followed Grandma to the door. "But what will we say to him?"

Grandma turned to face her. "There isn't anything we can say, Carrie," Grandma answered quietly.

Her words made Carrie feel almost unbearably sad. She longed to throw herself into Grandma's arms, but instead she took a deep breath and followed her outside to where the CCC boys had set the parlor furniture in a row along the fence. She sat close to Grandma on the sofa, near Grandpa's chair.

The three of them watched silently as the CCC boys carried out the curtains and the clothes that had been hanging in the closets. They were dragging some of the things along the ground, but that didn't seem important enough to mention.

Two men carried out a mirror and the pictures that had hung on the walls, and when they set them down, Carrie saw something slip to the ground. It was the calendar from her room, the one she and Amanda had used to count the number of Sunday visits they'd have during the summer. How long ago that seemed!

Carrie had the strange feeling that all this was happening to somebody else. That it was happening to somebody she didn't even know. Finally she asked, "Did they take you to jail, Grandpa?"

Her grandfather shook his head. "They took me to talk to the judge who signed the eviction papers." It seemed like a long time before he went on. "The judge said the state has the power to take property from some of the people for the good of all the people as long as it pays a fair price. He even showed me a line in the Constitution that made it legal." He shook his head. "I can't believe our founding fathers ever meant a thing like this to happen."

Then he turned to Grandma. "The judge gave me this," he said, pulling a folded check out of his shirt pocket. "I guess I'd better keep it this time."

Carrie wondered why Grandpa's letter to the president hadn't helped them. Why didn't President Roosevelt write back? All the other officials did. Maybe he just hadn't had time yet. Or maybe he'd never gotten Grandpa's letter. He might have a secretary like that operator who'd tried to censor her phone call, a secretary who decided the president didn't have time to read letters from people who wanted favors.

The three of them sat on the parlor furniture for what seemed like hours to Carrie. Occasionally a fly buzzed around her head, but it was too much trouble to swat at it. At last the truck driver came over to talk to Grandpa.

"We've got the house cleared out now," he said. "Could you check and make sure we haven't missed anything?"

"Come on, Sarah. Let's do it and get it over with," Grandpa said wearily. He stood up and reached out toward Grandma, and when she took his hand he pulled her to her feet. Together, they walked slowly toward the house. Carrie followed, painfully aware that they'd forgotten about her. The back of her throat began to ache, and she willed herself not to cry.

How strange the house looked, empty. And how loud their footsteps sounded as they walked from room to room. Mechanically, Grandpa opened and closed all the cupboards and closets while Grandma stood silently beside him and Carrie trailed along behind them, wishing she hadn't come back in.

Outside again, Grandpa said to the driver, "Have a couple of your boys save me that mantelpiece. My grandfather carved it as a wedding present for my father and his bride. Amanda Wilt, her name was." He stared past the driver for a moment, then shook his head and went back to the chair where he'd been sitting.

Carrie and Grandma followed him and took their places on the sofa. No one said anything. Cars going past slowed while people craned their necks to stare at the furniture lining the highway.

Finally two CCC boys came out carrying the heavy chestnut mantelpiece and leaned it against the kitchen stove.

"Well, that's it," said the driver. "Have you folks decided where you're going to go?"

Grandpa stared at him blankly, but Grandma said, "Our daughter in the valley is going to put us up, but her husband will need a little time to make room for our things."

The man nodded. "We can deliver them tomorrow, then."

Suddenly they heard Sport barking frantically and saw two of the CCC boys hurrying around the house.

"Some of us were going to clear out the toolshed, but your dog won't let us near it, sir," one of them called to Grandpa. "And we don't know what do with all them chickens."

Grandpa turned to Carrie. "Bring Sport around here while your Grandma and I decide what to do about her hens."

Half an hour later, Grandpa was tying the last crate of unhappy chickens to the car roof, and Sport lay panting on the floor of the back seat. Drops of moisture fell from his tongue and made little streaks where they rolled across Carrie's dusty feet.

"I'll personally make sure that all your tools are packed, Mr. Griffin," the driver said, extending his hand toward Grandpa.

Grandpa gave the man's hand a perfunctory shake and muttered, "I'd be much obliged to you for that."

No one spoke when Grandpa got in the car. As he pulled into the road, Carrie looked back and saw the CCC boys unloading cans of gasoline from their truck. Heartbroken, she bowed her head and wept.

26

Aunt Rose came to meet them when they arrived. Carrie climbed out of the car and Sport scrambled out behind her, but Grandma and Grandpa made no move to leave the front seat.

"Your hens look pretty miserable—better get them out of those crates and into my chicken yard," Aunt Rose said briskly.

Grandma and Grandpa seemed relieved to have someone tell them what to do. They climbed out of the car, and Grandpa began to untie the ropes that held the crates on the roof. The hens flapped their wings and clucked excitedly, and Grandma talked to them soothingly.

Carrie followed her aunt to the house, and as soon as they were inside, Aunt Rose turned to her and said, "Now tell me everything that happened."

"Oh, Aunt Rose, it was awful!" Carrie cried. And, her voice shaking, she began to describe the day's events, beginning with the arrival of the sheriff and his deputies and ending with a description of all their belongings lined up along the highway.

"Poor Dad," Aunt Rose said, shaking her head. "I was afraid it would come to that."

"And as soon as we left, the CCC boys poured gasoline all around and set everything on fire. So now there's nothing left of Grandma and Grandpa's house or the store or the lunchroom or any of the buildings out back, and the trunks of the poplar trees in the yard are all charred!"

Aunt Rose gathered Carrie into her arms and let her cry until there were no tears left. Finally, Carrie drew a long, shuddering breath. "Thanks for not saying 'I told you so,' Aunt Rose," she said.

"Believe me, this is one time I'd have gladly been wrong!" Aunt Rose wiped Carrie's face with her handkerchief. "Your cousins are on the far side of the pasture picking blueberries, so splash some cold water on your face and then run out there and tell them what's happened. And tell them not to say a word about any of this in front of their grandparents."

On her way out the kitchen door, Carrie saw Uncle George coming back from the field. He waved and headed toward the chicken yard, where Grandma and Grandpa were opening the last crate of hens. She heard him say, "So you lost the place, after all."

Grandpa didn't even look up. "I never thought something like this could happen in America," he said in a low voice.

Carrie hurried off to look for her cousins. She didn't want to hear anything more.

At breakfast the next morning Uncle George said, "I'll drive over to your place and tell the CCC boys how to get here. I've made room in the parlor to stack your mattresses and anything else mice could damage, and I've cleared space in the shed for the rest."

Grandpa nodded, and Carrie noticed that he had hardly touched his food.

"I might ride along with you, George, and get some beans out of the garden," said Grandma. "There should be ripe tomatoes, too."

Grandpa looked up. "You can't do that, Sarah," he said. "That's not your garden anymore. It's property of the Commonwealth of Virginia now, and I'll not have you trespassing on it."

Grandma opened her mouth as if to answer and then seemed to think better of it.

"Can we go with you in the truck?" asked Clarence.

"Please, Daddy?" begged little Benjamin, bouncing up and down in his chair.

"Sure you can," their father answered. "You girls want to come, too?"

Amanda looked hopefully at Carrie, but Carrie shook her head. She didn't want to see a charred ruin with a smoke-stained chimney rising out of it. "I'd rather stay here. We can play jacks," she said, remembering Amanda's disappointment when she discovered she'd forgotten to bring her jacks the week she visited.

After breakfast, Grandpa sat on one of the porch chairs, his hands folded in his lap. Sport came and put his head on his master's knee, but Grandpa just stared straight ahead of him with dull eyes. Carrie kept stealing glances at him, but he didn't even seem to notice that she and Amanda were there.

The girls played quietly. The only sounds were the bouncing of the ball on the porch floor and the jangle of the metal jacks. Carrie was pleased to find that she could still beat Amanda. She hadn't played since last summer—her friends in the city thought they were too old for jacks. She concentrated on the game, trying to pretend that this was just her usual end-of-summer visit with her cousins.

They were on their third game when Grandma and Aunt Rose came out of the house and Aunt Rose said, "We're going to walk up the road a little way. Why don't you girls come along?" Carrie was about to say she'd rather finish her jacks game, but when she saw the bright look on Grandma's face, she quickly got to her feet. She wanted to find out what was going on. "We can play later, Amanda," she said.

"Remember that we're on the threezies and it's my turn," Amanda said, gathering up the jacks and dropping them into their little drawstring bag.

"It's just half a mile up the road," Aunt Rose was saying as they closed the gate behind them. "The house has been empty for a while, so it will need some work. And the place is all overgrown with brambles and weeds."

Carrie looked from one woman to the other. What was her aunt talking about?

"That sounds like exactly what I want. It'll give your father something to do," Grandma said.

Maybe Aunt Rose had found a new place for Grandma and Grandpa! Carrie was so busy listening that it was a minute or two before she realized her cousin had gone on ahead. "Wait up, Amanda!" she called. "Wait for me!"

"Remember, now, not a word about that place. I'll tell Grandpa about it myself when the time is right," Grandma reminded the girls on the walk back to the farm.

Amanda quickly promised, but Carrie didn't bother to answer. She wasn't even tempted to tell about the square, ordinary-looking log house with its sagging front porch and its rooms full of cobwebs and mouse droppings. How could Grandma want to live there?

They were almost home when Uncle George's truck passed them, with the little boys waving excitedly from the cab.

"Looks like he's brought some of our stuff," said Carrie. "Come on, Amanda, let's go see."

She peered into the truck bed. "He brought Grandpa's tools and the mantelpiece, and a lot of burlap sacks. I don't remember anything in sacks."

"These sacks are for your grandma," Uncle George said, swinging them down to the ground.

Carrie looked inside first one, then another. A smile spread across her face and she called excitedly, "Grandma! Come and see!"

Grandma hurried over. Uncle George grinned and said, "Some of the CCC boys got bored with their guard duty and harvested your garden for you. There's beans, and potatoes, and squash. And I've got a bushel basket of tomatoes up front."

"Bless those boys!" said Grandma. "I hated to think of all that food going to waste. Lord knows, the Commonwealth of Virginia wasn't about to eat it."

Wondering if it had been Tom's idea to pick the vegetables, Carrie went to join the others on the porch with Grandpa.

"I have something for you, Dad," Uncle George was saying. "The driver of that CCC truck said the corps could use all the flour and sugar and other foodstuff from the store. I totaled it up and he paid me for it." He pulled some bills from his pocket and held them out, but Grandpa didn't even raise his head. Finally, Grandma reached out and took the money.

Uncle George cleared his throat nervously and then went on. "If it's all right with you, Dad, I'll have the auctioneer in town take care of the rest of your store goods, and the tables and other things from the lunchroom, too." Uncle George paused, and after a long time Grandpa nodded.

"Whatever you think's best, George," he said, his voice a monotone. Sport, who had been lying with his head on Grandpa's foot, looked up at his master with mournful eyes.

Uncle George pulled a handkerchief out of his pocket and wiped his face. "We'll keep the cash register in case you decide to open a store somewhere else."

"Let the auctioneer have it, too," Grandpa said. "I'm too old to open a new store."

Carrie caught her breath. Too old? Grandpa?

Uncle George looked at Grandma and raised his eyebrows, and Carrie saw her grandmother mouth the words, "Keep the register."

Uncle George nodded and moved closer to Grandpa. "The CCC boys will bring your furniture this afternoon, but I brought your tools back with me, Dad," he said. "And I brought your mantelpiece. I know how much that means to you."

"That was good of you," Grandpa said without looking up.

"Guess I'll store it all on the back porch so your tools don't get mixed up with mine," Uncle George went on.

Carrie had never heard her uncle say so much at one time!

Aunt Rose stood up. "You can unload the truck while Amanda and I start dinner, George," she said. "Clarence can help you, and Benjamin can hold the screen door open on the porch. Mama, you and Carrie better move those sacks of vegetables into the pantry. We'll snap the beans later and start canning tomorrow."

Grandpa was left sitting alone as everyone hurried off to carry out Aunt Rose's instructions. "Why don't you tell Grandpa about the new house?" Carrie asked as she followed Grandma across the yard. "Maybe that would cheer him up." She longed for him to be the person he used to be, the person he was before all this park business started.

Grandma shook her head. "He's not ready to be cheered up yet," she said. "He needs time to accept what's happened and time to get used to it. It'll be a while yet before I tell him about the new place."

"But I'll be going home in less than two weeks. Will he need more time than that?"

"I don't know, Carrie. He might."

It wasn't fair, Carrie thought as she picked up a sack of green beans and started back to the house. She didn't want to see Grandpa sitting slumped in the porch chair, and she didn't want to watch him silently pushing the food around his plate at mealtime for the rest of her visit. It would be terrible to remember him like that all during the long year ahead. And then it struck her: How was she going to get through the year with no summer memories to dream about and no more Blue Ridge Mountain summers to look forward to?

27

Carrie drained her milk glass and let her glance travel around the table. Amanda had saved the icing from her cake for last and was savoring it in tiny bites. Uncle George was vigorously stirring sugar into his iced tea. Clarence and Benjamin were quietly jabbing each other with their elbows, keeping angelic expressions on their faces all the while. Grandma was trying unsuccessfully to refuse the second helping of cake Aunt Rose had cut for her, and Grandpa . . . Resentfully, Carrie looked away from him. How dare he sit there day after day like—like a lump. She scowled and pushed aside her unfinished dessert.

"What's the matter, Carrie?" Aunt Rose asked. "Aren't you feeling well?"

Before Carrie could answer, Grandma said, "She looks like she could use some fresh air. If you don't mind, Rose, the two of us will go outside for a while."

Carrie looked up in surprise and found everyone's eyes on her. "Go with your grandma, Carrie. We can't have you feeling poorly," said Grandpa. It was the first time he'd spoken during the meal.

Embarrassed by all the attention, and a little ashamed of her anger at Grandpa, Carrie left the table and followed Grandma outside. She knew Grandma didn't think she was sick, and she steeled herself for a lecture.

But instead Grandma pointed to the lavender-blue flowers of the chickory growing along the dirt road outside the gate. "Let's pick a few of those," she said.

"I'll get some of that Queen Anne's lace," Carrie said, starting toward the tall blooms swaying in the breeze a short distance away. They looked like dainty white parasols, she thought as she leaned over to pick the flowers, or maybe like those crocheted antimacassars on the arms and back of Mama's sofa. For the first time, Carrie found herself almost looking forward to going home.

She glanced back and saw Grandma picking black-eyed Susans and goldenrod on the opposite side of the road. All the late summer flowers were pretty, but Carrie decided to make her bouquet all Queen Anne's lace. Moving from patch to patch, with the sun warm on her back and birds singing all around, she felt her anger begin to drain away, leaving in its place a tired sadness. Mama was right—this certainly hadn't been her usual carefree summer. The park business had ruined it—and now it had ruined everything, for all of them.

Carrie turned at the sound of Grandma's voice behind her. "Let's rest a while on the front steps before we go back."

To her surprise, Carrie saw that they'd walked all the way to the house Aunt Rose had showed them, and she thought how lonely it looked, standing empty in its weedy yard. "I'm going to run and get a bottle I saw a little way down the road," she said suddenly. "I'll fill it at the well out back and decorate the porch with my flowers."

"Good," said Grandma. "I see a rusty can to put mine in."

A few minutes later, the two bouquets were arranged on either side of the front door, and Carrie and Grandma were sitting on the porch steps. "Well, Sunshine, do you want to tell me what was bothering you at dinner?" Grandma asked.

Carrie swallowed hard. She'd hoped Grandma had forgotten about that. Then she took a deep breath and said, "I just couldn't stand the way Grandpa was acting."

Grandma gave her a long, steady look. "Grandpa wasn't *acting* that way, Carrie. Grandpa *is* that way."

Carrie frowned, not quite sure what her grandmother meant.

"You're thinking of yourself, you know, Carrie. At dinnertime, you weren't upset because your grandpa was unhappy. You were upset because of how it made you feel to see him 'acting unhappy.' "

For a moment, Carrie just stared at Grandma. Then she buried her face in her hands. How could she have been so selfish?

"He'll get over it, Carrie," Grandma said, putting her arm around Carrie and drawing her close. "But it'll take time. You have to accept that."

Carrie's voice was muffled. "I just want everything to be the way it used to be."

"You know that's impossible!" Grandma sounded exasperated. "Things will never be the same, Carrie. The old place is gone. Our old life is gone. And a lot of your grandpa's faith in himself is gone, too." She sighed. "I don't think he ever really doubted that he'd be able to save that place."

"But you knew he couldn't," Carrie said, remembering how she'd felt when she first realized that.

"I know how shocked you were when I let the appraiser come while Claude was at the bank. I was sorry to have to involve you in that, but . . . " Her voice faded away.

"That's okay, Grandma," Carrie assured her. "I didn't like having to show him around and answer his questions, but I knew it was important." She paused and then admitted, "I still don't feel quite right about it, though."

Grandma said, "Well, it was the only thing to do. I didn't think for one minute the government would change its plans for the national park on account of us. But your grandpa's a fighter. He had to fight till the end for what he thought was right. That's just the way he is."

Grandpa's a fighter. Carrie tried to remember when she'd first heard those words. Why, it was the day Molly Hughes had stopped by the lunchroom. *Your grandpa's a fighter*, Grandma had said, her words burning themselves into Carrie's memory. *You'll not be cutting him down from any barn rafters. He'll grieve awhile and then he'll get on with his life.*

"Is Grandpa grieving now?" Carrie asked.

Grandma nodded.

"When do you think he'll be ready to get on with his life?"

"It's hard to say, Carrie. But by the time you come next summer, he should be his old self again." Grandma stood up. "Now let's go in and decide which bedroom will be yours."

This time the old house seemed more welcoming. They climbed the stairs, and Carrie looked in first one room and then another. She knew at once which she wanted— the one in the southeast corner with views of the Blue Ridge from both windows.

Carrie turned to Grandma. "Amanda and I can come over tomorrow and sweep the place out and maybe wash the windows."

Grandma gave her a squeeze. "Wonderful! I didn't know how I'd find time to spruce things up a bit before I showed it to your grandpa, with all those vegetables to put up."

"That's something I don't understand," Carrie said slowly. "*You* aren't sitting around, not talking or eating.

You're canning beans and tomatoes with Aunt Rose and planning how to fix up this old house. But you must feel just as unhappy as Grandpa does."

Grandma walked to the window and stood looking toward the mountains. Finally she said, "I'm sorry all this happened. Deeply sorry. But I expected it would end like this, and it's a relief to have it settled. And staying busy keeps me from brooding over what can't be helped."

"Maybe being busy would keep Grandpa from brooding, too."

"Why do you think I want us to buy this rundown old house?" Grandma asked, leading the way downstairs.

As they walked back to the farm, Carrie imagined Grandpa and Grandma working together to turn the neglected house into a home and the weedy, overgrown area around it into a grassy yard and productive garden. When she came next summer, she wouldn't recognize the place! But her room would have the familiar furniture and rag rug, and her favorite quilt would be on the bed. Grandma would have a vase of flowers on the bureau, too, just like she always did. And best of all, Carrie thought, next year she'd be able to see Amanda every day instead of just every other Sunday and a week at the end of summer.

"Carrie! Do you see what I see? By the gate!" Grandma pointed down the road ahead of them.

Shading her eyes with her hand, Carrie saw Grandpa leaning on Aunt Rose's gate and waving to them. Carrie waved back, and Grandpa started slowly toward them.

"Where have you two been?" he asked gruffly. "I was worried about you."

"We were just picking wildflowers, Grandpa."

"Wildflowers? I don't see any wildflowers."

Carrie and Grandma looked at each other. "I guess we forgot to bring them," Carrie said, giggling nervously.

"Something strange is going on here," Grandpa said, looking accusingly from one of them to the other.

"Don't worry, Claude. Everything's going to be all right," Grandma said, slipping her arm through his.

Everything *was* going to be all right, Carrie thought as she walked to the house behind her grandparents. But she wished she knew when.

28

Aunt Rose stood in front of Grandpa, hands on her hips, and announced, "You've been sitting like this for almost two weeks, Dad, and that's long enough. Carrie's leaving tomorrow, and I want you to take her to town and buy her some shoes for school."

Carrie held her breath, waiting to see what would happen, and to her relief, Grandpa slowly got up and reached in his pocket for his car keys.

"Come on, Carrie," he said. "Let's go get you ready for school." He sounded resigned.

Grandpa didn't say much on the trip to town, but once there, he was more like the person Carrie remembered, stopping to chat with everyone he knew. Shopping seemed to take forever, with all the interruptions, but at last they started back to the car, carrying a bag full of school supplies as well as the new shoes.

But to Carrie's dismay, Grandpa met still another acquaintance on the way. She shifted her weight from one foot to the other, wondering how long he was going to stand there talking. He'd told the story of losing the place over and over, and whenever he'd finish, his listener would sigh and say, "Well, I was afraid that's how it would end." And Grandpa would say, "Well, I sure didn't think it would end that way. And neither did Carrie. She was behind me a hundred percent, weren't you, Sunshine?" And then she was expected to look up and smile and nod her head.

But each time, she felt a little worse. Would Grandpa be telling people she'd been behind him a hundred percent if he knew she'd shown the appraiser around? Carrie wondered why that bothered her so much now, of all times. Helping Grandma prepare for the worst had certainly been the right thing to do—after all, the worst had happened, hadn't it? So if she hadn't done anything wrong, why did she feel so guilty? It must be because she was "operating under false pretenses," as Mama would say.

At last they started toward the car again, and Carrie hoped they wouldn't meet anyone else Grandpa knew before they got there. She'd liked it better other years when they'd chosen her school shoes and pencils and notebooks from Grandpa's store. Her heart fell when she saw a thin little woman hurrying purposefully toward them.

"You remember Mrs. Stokes, don't you, Carrie?" Grandpa said after he greeted the woman.

The telephone operator she'd hung up on! Carrie

wanted to shrink out of sight, but instead she made herself smile and say, "Good afternoon, Mrs. Stokes."

"Did you ever get through to the president, dear?" the woman asked, smiling sweetly.

"No, ma'am, but my grandfather wrote a letter to him."

Mrs. Stokes' eyebrows rose in two thin curves and her mouth formed a perfect O. "Imagine that!" she exclaimed. Then she looked up at Grandpa and said, "It didn't do any good, though, did it, Claude?"

Before he could answer, Carrie said, "It didn't help us keep the place, but at least Grandpa knows he fought a good fight. Don't you think that's important, Mrs. Stokes?"

"Why, I guess I never really thought about it," she said slowly.

Back at the old Dodge at last, Carrie rolled down her window and leaned back, glad for a chance to rest her feet.

"So you think I fought a good fight, do you?" Grandpa asked as he started the car. "I was worried that you were disappointed in me because I lost the place."

"I could never be disappointed in you, Grandpa. How could I possibly be, when you stood up for what you believed in? And you really did fight a good fight."

"Well, if you can't win, I guess that's next best."

Neither of them said much on the rest of the ride home, but as they neared the farm Grandpa said, "It's probably time Sarah and I started looking for a new place. We seem to be wearing out our welcome here."

"I guess you didn't like what Aunt Rose said this afternoon." Carrie grinned in spite of herself, remembering.

"That was no way for a daughter to talk to her father," Grandpa grumbled, slowing down as he approached a curve.

"Well, I'm glad she said it. It really was time for you to get out of that porch chair." Carrie was surprised she was able to tell Grandpa that. When he turned and scowled at her, she said, "I *missed* you, Grandpa," and his face relaxed into a smile.

"Want to play jacks?" Amanda asked the next afternoon.

Carrie shook her head. "Well, what do you want to do? You don't have to leave for hours and hours."

Carrie hesitated a moment before she said, "What I really want to do is go for a walk with Grandpa, just the two of us."

"He's out back with Daddy," Amanda said, jumping up. "I'll get him for you."

Carrie watched Amanda hurry around the house. Ever since yesterday she'd been hoping for a chance to talk to Grandpa alone, but now she felt uneasy. He wasn't going to like what she had to say, but she'd feel guilty all year long if she didn't tell him.

Sport came bounding up, followed by Amanda and Grandpa. "Well, Sunshine," Grandpa said, "I hear you're going to take Sport and me for a walk."

Carrie nodded, and they set off, with Sport running ahead of them, sniffing at the weeds along the roadside.

"Your cousin said there was something you wanted to ask me," Grandpa said at last.

Carrie took a deep breath. "Not exactly. There's something I have to tell you."

"Something you *have* to tell me. Not something you *want* to tell me?"

Carrie nodded. "Do you remember the day I brought your check from the state up from the post office?"

"Sure do. I'll never forget how I felt when I saw it."

Carrie looked up. "How did you feel, Grandpa?"

"I had all different kinds of feelings mixed up together. I was shocked at how fast the Commonwealth of Virginia was moving to buy the land. And I was surprised at how much the check was for. And I wondered who told them enough about the place that they were paying so much more than I'd heard mountain land was going for." He shook his head. "Hugh Edwards is the only one I figure might have done it. He was pretty sore at me."

"I'm the one who did it, Grandpa," Carrie said in a small voice.

Grandpa stopped short. "*You?*"

Carrie nodded. "Grandma asked me to show the appraiser around one Thursday morning while you were in town."

"But I thought—but you always seemed so sure I'd be able to keep the place!"

"I *was* sure, Grandpa!"

"Then why—"

"It was like insurance, Grandpa." When he looked down at her with a puzzled expression on his face, Carrie hurried on. "Just like Daddy has life insurance even though he doesn't think he's going to die—it's so he doesn't have to worry about what would happen to Mama and me if he did."

Grandpa nodded thoughtfully. "Insurance," he said. "Insurance." He pulled his handkerchief out of his pocket to wipe his face, and Carrie noticed how tired he looked.

"Maybe we should sit down and rest a while," she said, trying not to let her concern show in her voice.

He agreed quickly. "I guess your grandpa's not as young as he used to be."

"I guess my grandpa's just been sitting around and hardly eating anything for almost two weeks," Carrie retorted.

"Hrmmph," said Grandpa. "I guess I'd rather be thought old than lazy. But then, lazy I can do something about."

"Nobody thinks you're lazy, Grandpa," Carrie said quickly. "We know you're grieving. But you're ready to get on with your life now, aren't you?" she asked hopefully.

"I'm ready for a little rest. Come on, we can sit on the steps of that empty house."

Carrie gulped. They shouldn't have walked so far. Grandma had wanted to be the one to show Grandpa the new place!

Grandpa bent to examine the broken gate and then straightened up to look at the house. "This must have been a fine old home once," he said. "Look at the size of those squared logs!"

Carrie sat down on the steps, with Sport panting beside her, but Grandpa went up onto the sagging porch, carefully testing the boards before he put his full weight on them. "Come and rest, Grandpa," she said, but he opened the front door and went inside. Carrie sat on the porch, waiting. What was he doing in there so long? She looked at the afternoon shadows and tried to guess what time it was. What if she missed her train? Her heart began to beat faster.

At last Grandpa came out. "Well, Sunshine," he said, "we'd better start back so we can get you to the station."

"But you haven't had your rest," Carrie objected.

"I don't feel tired anymore," he said, smiling down at her. "Let's go."

As Sport trotted down the dusty road ahead of them, Carrie noticed that Grandpa was walking much faster than he had earlier.

"Are you afraid we're going to be late?" she asked anxiously.

"We have plenty of time, Sunshine." They were half-way home when Grandpa slowed his steps a little and said, "You know, there was something odd about that old house."

Carrie frowned. "Odd?"

He nodded. "It must have been years since anyone lived there, and yet I didn't see a bit of dust or a single cobweb. And the windows sparkled like they'd just been washed." He paused. "But the strangest thing of all was a big bouquet of wildflowers in one of the upstairs rooms. The room that faces the mountains."

Carrie didn't know what to say. Grandpa smiled at her, his eyes twinkling. "I think you women have been keeping something from me."

"Oh, Grandpa, it was supposed to be a surprise—Grandma wanted to be the one to show you that house!"

"She will be. She'll show it to me, and I'll say I think we ought to buy it and fix it up." He walked a few steps more. "And do you know how we'll pay for it?"

Carrie shook her head.

"With your insurance money, Sunshine. With your insurance money."

Carrie tried to wipe the train window clean with her handkerchief, but most of the dirt was on the outside. Through the grimy glass she could barely make out her grandparents, standing side by side, waving to her as the train pulled out of the station. She waved back, hoping they could see her, and then she closed her eyes, trying to fix that last glimpse of them in her mind. She wanted to remember them like that, not staring solemnly out at her from the pictures on Mama's bureau.

In just a few hours she'd be back in the city. Summer was over, and school would start on Monday. Carrie thought of the new dresses Grandma had made for her and the shoes and school supplies Grandpa had bought her in town the day before. She was ready for classes to start. But then she felt the little stirrings of nervousness that were always part of the beginning of a new school year: What if the teacher was mean? What if the work was too hard? What if the kids thought they could push her around because she was small and quiet? What if—

"All ready for school?" the conductor asked, stopping beside her.

"I sure am," Carrie said, handing him her ticket.

Had she really said that? she wondered as he moved on to the next passenger. And then she realized that she *was* ready—ready to face the new school year, whatever it brought. After all, it couldn't be as hard as her summer had been. She leaned back and shut her eyes again as a wave of sadness swept over her. Having to leave the mountain was just about the worst thing that could have happened. But she'd lived through it, and so had her grandparents. Even Grandpa seemed almost himself again.

She wasn't going to worry about school—or anything else. And this year, she'd face up to her problems instead of daydreaming about summer in the Blue Ridge every time something went wrong. From now on, she was going to be a fighter, just like Grandpa. Or maybe she'd be like Grandma instead, and quietly do whatever had to be done. Or like her no-nonsense aunt—but then, she couldn't quite imagine telling everyone else what to do. She smiled at the thought.

No, she would just be herself. Her *new* self, that is— the person she'd become during her last summer on Grandpa's mountain.